the rules of persuasion

the rules of persuasion

AMITY HOPE

Entangled Publishing, LLC
2614 South Timberline Road
Suite 109
Fort Collins, CO 80525
Visit our website at www.entangledpublishing.com.

Crush is an imprint of Entangled Publishing, LLC.

Edited by Stacy Abrams and Alexa May
Cover design by Cover Couture
Cover art from DepositPhotos

Manufactured in the United States of America

First Edition July 2017

For my boys, Zack and Nick. I'm so proud of you both. I'm so blessed to be your mom. I know your dad is watching over you, every bit as proud of you as I am.

Chapter One

MEG

I slowly backed away from Laurel High School. My footsteps were nearly soundless, courtesy of the thick soles on my motorcycle boots. With every step I took, my most recent creation became a little more lost in the shadows. I hitched my backpack higher up my shoulder, the cans of spray paint rattling around. The little metal balls inside each can clanged, creating a raucous melody.

The brick wall was my canvas, but to say I was an artist was a stretch. To call my work a masterpiece was blasphemy. Still, my signature piece—my only piece—was improving with every rendition.

Light from the streetlamps didn't reach nearly this far. Our school was on the edge of town in a quiet neighborhood. It was set back from the street, laced in by a row of hedges. I was able to work in relative privacy. Of course, it helped that at this time of night most everyone was asleep.

I paused for a moment to press my fingertips to my lips,

then closed my eyes and blew the kiss up into the starry sky, willing it to reach the heavens. As always, I felt as if another little chunk of the weight holding me down floated away with it. It was why I did this—not every night, but often enough. Painting was cathartic.

Another step backward landed me against something solid. Solid with a bit of give. I knew instinctively I hadn't bumped into some*thing* but rather some*one*. I reflexively lurched forward, losing my balance as my boot nicked the raised edge of the sidewalk. An arm whipped around me and tugged me backward, caging me in. I sucked in a breath, ready to scream.

His free hand clamped over my mouth to muffle the sound.

I tried to pull my elbow back to get in at least one good jab, but his arm was still looped around me, pinning my body to his. I tried to suck in another deep breath, but his hand remained over my mouth.

"Hey. Don't scream. You don't want everyone looking out their windows, do you?" His voice sounded frantic, as frantic as my own clanging heart.

Did I? Probably. Then someone could call the police to get this crazy guy off me. I did the only thing I could think of. I lifted my feet, forcing him to support all my weight with the single arm he had around me. It worked and nearly toppled us both.

"Damn." He dropped me to the ground, not letting go completely. His hand fell from my mouth, joining his other hand around my waist, trying to steady me as we stumbled.

"I'm not going to hurt you," he said. "*You* crashed into *me*. I was trying to keep you upright when you decided to yell."

I regained my footing as his hands slid away. He was only feet from me, but with the streetlight behind him, his face was nothing more than a silhouette. I backed away and he followed. The movement pulled him from the light and into the shadows, where, ironically, I could see him better.

I groaned.

I knew this guy.

He narrowed his eyes at me, and in that instant I knew he was trying to place me as well.

Lightning fast, he reached for me. I tried to swat his hand away, but in my shocked stupor I was a second too slow, and he pulled the black knit cap from my head.

My face was average, fairly unremarkable. But my hair? It was what everyone remembered about me. Long and auburn, it cascaded to my elbows in bouncy waves. It was my best feature and right now, as it tumbled from beneath my cap to shimmer in the dim lighting, it was a traitorous one.

He dangled my cap in front of me. I quickly swiped it out of his hand.

"So this is what the mysterious Meg Matthews does in her free time." His tone held a hint of gloating.

I was hardly mysterious. If he didn't know a thing about me, it was because we drifted in different social circles. He was neck deep in the crowd that thought they ruled the school. I was perfectly happy being part of a trio that floated around the fringes.

He was staring past me, checking out my mural. "It looks even better up close."

I was tempted to kick him in the family jewels so I could make a run for it. *That*, I knew, would wipe the smug, knowing look off his face. But it was probably a very bad idea to mess with the Prescott family's precious jewels, both literally and figuratively speaking.

The Prescotts were one of the wealthiest families in town. His dad was the Prescott in Prescott & Holbrook, the prestigious law firm that was notorious for representing corporations of questionable standing. Everyone in town knew to never cross the Prescotts.

It was best not to mess with this boy.

Making up my mind, I sidestepped him and took off at a pace that was not quite a run. He darted in front of me. I let out an embarrassingly loud yelp as I nearly slammed into him for the second time in a matter of minutes.

"Whoa, slow down," he ordered. "Where do you think you're going?"

"Home." I shrugged.

I tried to take another step, but he blocked my way again. For several long seconds we did a sloppy dance of darting and dodging. Tired of our charade, I stopped and looked up into his eyes.

I straightened my spine and squared my shoulders. I was taller than most of the girls at school. Still, I wasn't quite as tall as him, even in my heeled boots. That didn't matter. I wasn't going to let him intimidate me.

"Get out of my way, Luke."

"Not quite yet."

"*Excuse me*? Are you going to stop me?" I hoped my voice wasn't quaking the same way my insides were.

A wicked look of amusement flashed across his face.

"I'm out of here." I shoved past him. The traitorous cans of paint banged together. The sound echoed in my ears.

He grabbed me by the wrist and pulled me to a stop. His fingers held tightly enough to be a warning, but not enough to hurt.

"What?" I snapped.

"I caught you vandalizing a building. I think you better be a little nicer to me." His tone was soft, friendly. Fake.

I snorted out an indignant laugh. "Is that a threat? And you didn't catch me doing anything."

"Are you sure about that?" he taunted.

"You don't know that I did anything wrong. Maybe I was just walking by. In fact, I *was* just walking by."

He reached around me and gave my backpack a nudge. The metal paint cans clinked together again, announcing my guilt. Damn those cans of paint and their telltale rattling.

He smirked.

I gritted my teeth.

He snatched up my right hand and held it between both of his. The soft glow of the streetlamp made the drying paint stand out like crusty blood on my fingers.

He laughed. "I have literally caught you red-handed."

My heart hammered so hard it ached in my chest.

His grip loosened. It was his words that held me in place now. "Not to mention I was watching you. From right over there." He motioned toward the row of hedges that edged the school lawn.

"Really?" I scoffed. "Who would've guessed Luke Prescott has a fetish for creeping on girls."

He shook his head, that smug smile making my blood sizzle. "Uh-uh. You're not turning this around on me. Not when you're the one breaking the law."

"So…what? You're going to tattle on me?" I crossed my arms over my chest, clenching my fists in an attempt to keep my hands from shaking.

We were only a week into senior year. I'd get suspended for this, more than likely expelled. Not to mention any charges the police would press.

In the past year I'd tagged maybe a dozen buildings, sidewalks, and other random surfaces…and I'd never been caught. I hated to admit it, but the truth was that when I had a can of paint in my hand, I felt invincible.

I had more riding on this than Luke knew.

He looked over my head and eyed my work again. He chewed on his lip, giving the impression that he was mulling things over. I was sure it was all for show. He clearly knew exactly what his answer was going to be.

He wanted me to squirm.

Well, I wouldn't do it. Not for him.

I let out what I hoped was a bored-sounding sigh. He probably expected me to wait all night for him. He was the kind of guy who was spoiled, entitled, used to getting what he wanted. He had gorgeous cornflower blue eyes and golden hair that curled up at the edges of his ball cap. His dimples would've made him look angelic if it weren't for the smile that was so devilish. He looked just innocent enough to be dangerous.

"Tell ya what," he said. "Let's make a deal. I'll keep this quiet, but you'll owe me a favor."

I grimaced as his eyes scanned over me. I was wearing black leggings and a black long-sleeve fitted T-shirt. Under Luke's scrutiny the form-fitting duo felt oddly promiscuous.

"No."

"You really aren't in the position to refuse me."

"And yet," I said, "that's exactly what I intend to do."

"You sure are feisty." It sounded suspiciously like a compliment. "How can you be so sure you'll say no? You don't even know what the favor is."

"Then enlighten me."

He shrugged. "I don't know yet. I'm working on it."

My face crinkled in confusion. "Working on it?"

He tapped his head with two fingers. "Working on it."

"Right." I took off.

He fell into step beside me. His running shoes quickly matched the rhythm of my boots. One look at him and it was pretty clear what he'd been up to. He was wearing athletic shorts and a faded baseball T-shirt. Now that my intense panic had ebbed into a feeling of minor trepidation, I could make out the faded scent of his cologne mingled with a subtle hint of sweat.

I stopped.

So did he.

"What are you *doing*?" I demanded. "Don't you have a midnight run to finish?"

He made a face at me, as if the answer was obvious, and said, "I'm walking you home. Come on." He held out his hand, probably expecting me to melt at the gesture, like a snowflake in his palm. I was no flake. There would be no melting on my part.

I took a step back, and he dropped his hand to his side.

"You know where I live?" I asked incredulously.

"No," he grinned. "I figured you'd lead the way."

I was unfairly thrown by his smirk and the repeat appearance of his dimples. I stared at him stupidly for a moment before regaining my senses.

"I don't need you to walk me home." I made a shooing motion with my fingers. "Go away."

"Not happening." He crossed his arms over his chest and stared me down.

"What? Why? It's not enough that you harassed me, bullied me, and threatened me? Now you're going to stalk me, too?"

He looked around, motioning to our surroundings. We had reached the sidewalk that lined the deserted street. "It's late. It's dark. You're a girl."

"And you're sexist."

He snorted. "Hardly. I couldn't live with myself if something happened to you because I was too lazy to see you home."

"Are you serious right now? This is Laurel!" Our northern California town was quiet, idyllic. It was far enough inland to deter tourists but close enough to the Pacific to make weekend picnics at the coast ideal. "*Nothing* happens here!"

"Says Laurel's most top-secret criminal." He nodded sagely.

I ignored his sarcasm. "You don't have to walk me home."

"I do."

"Actually," I pointed down the street, "you don't." The silhouette of my Honda Rebel was visible within the shadows of a dogwood tree. The leaves rustled in the autumn breeze. "I'm driving. I'll get home just fine. Thank you." My tone relayed anything but thankfulness.

"Awesome motorcycle," he murmured reverentially. "Will you give me a ride?"

I raised an eyebrow. "Is that the favor you want?"

He frowned. "No."

"Then, *no*." I smiled sweetly back at him. "I'm going to go now. Got it?"

He didn't stop me as I scurried away from him. Instead his voice floated across the distance I'd covered.

"Don't worry, Meg. I'll keep in touch."

I quickened my pace.

It felt as if I took forever to cover the distance to my Rebel. The moment I did I felt a wave of relief spill through me. Hopefully Luke was all talk and I would never have to think of this night again. I tossed my leg over the side, yanked my helmet on, and moments later my bike roared to life.

My metallic blue baby was hardly ideal for a stealthy getaway. That's why I always parked several blocks away. The machine rumbled beneath me, familiar and comforting. With a nudge of the throttle, it would whisk me away from here.

I dared a glance over my shoulder before I took off. Luke was standing right where I'd left him, his arms crossed over his chest. One hand listlessly tapped against a sculpted bicep. He gazed at me with an intensity that made me tremble.

A favor? I couldn't imagine what that boy could ever want from me.

Chapter Two

MEG

I ducked into a classroom when I saw our guidance counselor, Miss Perez, strolling in my direction. As always she wore an immaculate pantsuit, kitten heels, and a dainty string of pearls. Her glossy black hair was snipped into a flawless bob. She looked like she belonged in a private practice office. Not a cramped, windowless cubicle that harbored the smells of teachers' lunches nuked in the break room across the hall.

Shortly after Sydney's terminal diagnosis three years ago, my parents insisted I meet with someone to help me cope. It was too bad they didn't abide by the same rule. While I missed my little sister beyond measure, at least I was able to get out of bed in the morning. I hadn't cut myself off from my friends or retreated into a shell of my former self. Not like my mother had. And my father? He had thrown himself so totally and completely into his business that we hardly saw him anymore.

I had crept through the front door last night, not at all surprised to find Mom sleeping on the couch. I made my way up the stairs to the sound of Dad's soft, rumbling snores. He always slept with the bedroom door open—no matter how bad of a fight they had—a standing invitation for my mother to join him.

She never did.

As far as I knew she hadn't slept in their bed since Sydney died.

The *clickety-clack* of Miss Perez's heels grew louder, and then the sound receded as she passed by.

Most days I wouldn't even consider avoiding her. Today was a different story. Miss Perez could read me easier than her favorite psychology text. One look at my face and she'd likely know I'd gotten myself into trouble last night.

I eased back into the crowded hallway.

I hadn't been able to sleep after last night's excitement, so I'd gotten up early. I took advantage of the extra time by coating myself in imaginary armor. My eyeliner was a little thicker, my eye shadow a little darker.

I'd slipped into my favorite boots. They were black, up to my knees, with silver buckles down the sides. The spiked heels gave my height enough of a boost that they should put me at eye level with Luke. I was anticipating a run in with him. I didn't want him to have any sort of advantage over me. Not even the advantage of height.

My leather pants were previously reserved solely for riding. My black sweater hung loosely off one shoulder. I hoped it screamed edgy. I wanted to give off a don't-mess-with-me vibe without coming across as totally tacky.

My best friend, Francesca Rossini, swooped in from behind me as I neared my locker. Her fingers dug into my biceps as she pulled me into an alcove. Francesca was petite, yet her temper could be monstrous.

"What were you thinking?" Her words were a hiss, her dark brown eyes alert as they scanned the hallway, making sure no one was listening. She shoved an unruly dark curl behind her ear. It defiantly bounced right back, landing against her olive-toned cheek.

Francesca was the only person I'd ever told about my late-night obsession.

She obviously didn't approve.

I couldn't blame her. If she knew the murals were in honor of Sydney, she'd probably be more understanding. But it hurt too much to talk about, so I'd never explained it, not even to her.

"I mean, the *school*? It's one thing to paint an abandoned building that no one is going to notice. It's another thing entirely to paint the freaking school." She jammed her fists onto her hips.

I pinched the bridge of my nose. "I know."

"What if someone had seen you? Do you know how much trouble—"

Her gaze zeroed in on something past my shoulder. I twisted around to see what had her so bewildered and found myself facing Luke. I couldn't remember if he was normally in this hallway in the morning.

He grinned at me like we were old pals.

"Hey, Meg. How's it going?"

I stuffed down a groan and fought the urge to give him the bird.

He continued to smile.

I glared back.

I felt Francesca's gaze swing between us.

He said, "Did you get home safely last night?"

"I obviously did," I replied through gritted teeth.

"So I stopped by the office this morning. I had to hand in some paperwork for a class I dropped. Principal Prichard is not a happy man right now. He's mad, Meg, real mad." Luke shook his head, attempting to look forlorn.

"Why would Meg care?" Francesca asked in a careful tone.

He looked at me and winked.

"What do you want, Luke?" I grumbled.

He shrugged. "Just wanted to say hi."

"Hi. Now go."

"So feisty." He chuckled as if this had become a joke between us.

"We have to get to class." Francesca grabbed my arm and tugged me away again.

I glanced back at him and made a face as if to say, *What can I do?*

His lips twitched in amusement.

"Last night?" Francesca's fingers dug into me as she towed me through the crowd.

"I ran into him. Last night."

We skidded to a stop as we reached my locker. She wedged her fists onto her hips again. It was a stance I knew well.

"Ah, *hell no*," she said. "He knows?"

I made an apologetic face and nodded.

"*He knows*?" she whisper-yelled this time.

"Yes."

"Meg. How did he find out?" Only a few beats passed before she grimaced. "He caught you?"

"Literally red-handed," I mumbled.

She narrowed her eyes at me and tossed her ebony mane of ringlets over her shoulder. Her silence was a testament to how angry she was.

"It's fine," I said emphatically. "I have it under control. He's not going to tell anyone."

"You'd better hope not." She spun on her heel and marched off to her locker without a backward glance.

. . .

"Okay. So, news flash." Kylie Jenkins dropped into the seat across from me. "Jaclyn Winters was talking about you in second hour. Bethany Hanson and Meredith Cooper are both in the class with us. Obviously she doesn't have a clue who I am so I was able to listen in on the whole conversation."

She looked at Francesca and me, vibrating with excitement.

I poked at the limp salad I'd assembled.

"What did she say?" Francesca momentarily set her cell phone down on the table. Typically she spent all of her lunch hour texting Nate, her boyfriend. He was off at college two hours away, but he came back to Laurel every weekend. During the week they texted, FaceTimed, and chatted on the phone every chance they got.

"She was super pissed because she said she's heard Luke's been asking around about Meg." Kylie turned to me as if I hadn't just heard her explanation. "Jaclyn wants to know why Luke is asking about you."

I wilted in my seat.

Kylie stared at me with blatant curiosity, her green eyes silently assessing. She leaned forward on her elbow, waiting for me to say something.

I didn't know what to say. I had no idea what Luke was up to.

Was he trying to see if I had a criminal past?

Maybe he *was* looking into me. Maybe he was curious about whether or not this was a one-time thing or if I had a history of unlawful behavior. Would he not keep my secret if he thought I was a repeat offender? I'd never been caught before. He wouldn't find out anything that way. But that didn't mean that he wouldn't be able to find my other murals himself. I rubbed my temples.

"So why," Kylie wondered as she began to peel her orange, "is Luke asking about you?"

"How should I know?" I stabbed a cucumber. This was getting more complicated by the second.

"Well, are you interested in him?" Kylie pressed as Francesca simultaneously chewed her food and mentally scolded me.

"Why would you ask that?" I demanded.

She leaned back in her seat. "Why do you think? It seems like he's interested in you. I wondered if—"

Francesca interjected, "No, Meg isn't interested in him."

"What she said," I agreed.

"But—"

"No, Kylie," I interrupted. "I have no interest in Luke Prescott. Nor do I have any interest in facing the wrath of Jaclyn Winters."

"They broke up."

"Who? Luke and Jaclyn?" I glanced around at my friends. Francesca nodded. I shrugged. "Doesn't matter."

"They broke up over summer break. How do you not know that?" Kylie asked.

"I think the question is *why would I care*?"

Kylie looked stumped. "I don't know. Maybe because he's the star pitcher for the Laurel Wildcats? They say he's so good he could possibly go pro if he wanted to. Or maybe because his dad practically owns this town? Or maybe—"

"Maybe you should drop it," Francesca ordered.

Kylie frowned. "What's with you two?"

"Nothing. Just tired," I said as I tried to smooth things over.

"Things not going well at home?" she asked.

"Are things ever good at home?"

"Good point. So maybe you should let him take your mind off things." She peeled another wedge from her orange.

"You're wrong. It's not like that."

"Tell him that."

Reflexively I followed her line of sight. It led to the most coveted table, the one closest to the door. The inhabitants never had to trudge their way through the maze that was the cafeteria. My gaze collided with Luke's. He grinned at me and had the nerve to wave.

"See what I mean?" Kylie asked.

"I'll be right back." I shoved away from the table and swerved my way through the crowded room. The closer I drew to Luke, the bigger — no, cockier — his grin got.

"Well, hello there, Meg Matthews," he said.

My gaze bounced around the table. His friends had stopped talking and were now eyeing me with curiosity. I forced a smile as I returned my attention to Luke. "We need to talk."

His chair slid across the gritty linoleum with a squeal. I headed toward the cafeteria doors, staying a few steps ahead of him. I didn't glance around, but anxiety danced up and down my spine as I imagined every eye in the room drilling into our backs. It was much quieter out in the hallway.

"What's up?" He leaned against a locker and cocked his head to the side, pale blue eyes sparkling with amusement. He looked harmless in his cozy cream-colored Henley. His deceptively charming dimples sprang to life as a smug smile crept onto his face.

"Stop asking around about me." I channeled Francesca and armed myself with some attitude. I slammed my fists onto my hips as I glared at him, eye to eye.

"That bothers you?"

"I didn't say it bothers me. I just don't like it."

"Well, you better get used to it."

"Why is that?"

"Meet me at Maebelle's Diner after school."

"Maebelle's?" It was a small diner on the edge of town. I knew it well. "No."

"I think you mean yes," he said calmly. "You did hear this morning's announcements, right? Mr. Prichard made it perfectly clear he wants the vandal caught."

My heart rate kicked up several notches. I *had* heard the morning announcements.

"I even heard rumors," Luke casually stated, "that the PTA is trying to scrounge up a rather substantial reward."

Students were loitering at the vending machines. Did he have to talk so loud?

"I'll be at Maebelle's. If you don't show by four o'clock, I'll be giving Mr. Prichard a visit."

"Can't you say whatever it is you're going to say? Save us both some time?" I fell back against the lockers and stared at the ceiling, the inevitability of the situation settling upon me.

"You owe me."

"So you've said."

He leaned in close, keeping his voice low. His nearness made my heart stutter. "You're going to pay me back by being my girlfriend."

I whipped my head toward him. *What the hell?* Surely I had heard him wrong. I waited for him to laugh. To tell me he was joking. When he didn't, I laughed instead.

"Um, no." I frantically glanced around, grateful our friends were still in the cafeteria. No one out here was paying attention to us. The students at the vending machine were more concerned with their junk food options.

A feeling of dread pooled in my stomach. I hadn't allowed myself to give much thought to what Luke would expect from me. But this? This was the *last* thing I would've dreamed of.

"*Fake* girlfriend," he amended. "It'll be for show."

"You are insane." I started backing away from him on wobbly legs. "There is no way I'm going to live that kind of lie."

"Why? Because you're so honorable?" He scoffed. "I caught you *vandalizing* school property. Don't take this the wrong way, but to me that says you're at least a little bit morally pliable." He winked at me. "Maebelle's. See you there."

With that, he pushed off from the locker and sauntered away.

I stared after him. I would not be anyone's fake girlfriend.

Chapter Three

LUKE

Gorgeous was the first word that came to mind when I thought of Meg. *Uptight* came in at a close second. She strode into Maebelle's, hips swaying, scowling as if she was angry at the world. More than likely she was just angry with me.

"You're late. And your malt is melting." I slid my paperback into my backpack but not before she caught a glimpse of the title.

"*The Handmaid's Tale*? Sounds scintillating. Or more like the sort of book a guy who creeps around in the bushes would read." She smirked down at me, refusing to take a seat.

"*Or*," I said, smirking back, "it's the sort of book one is forced to read for AP English. Given your lack of knowledge on the matter, I'm guessing you aren't cut out for AP classes."

Her mouth slammed into a frown, and I felt a stab of guilt. Had I offended her? She didn't seem like the sort of girl to take offense to much of anything. In fact, she seemed like the sort of girl who could hold her own in just about any situation.

I wasn't sure what was up with the all black, all the time. But she wore it well. Every inch of her, from her amazing red hair, the creamy shoulder peeking out from her sweater, the tight fit of her leather pants, to the sexy boots on her feet.

"What?" she snapped. She finally flopped into the seat across from me.

I pulled my eyes back up to her face. I hadn't meant to so blatantly check her out.

"I'm just trying to figure you out. You going for an emo look or something?"

She wrinkled her face at me.

"Ninja?"

She gave me an *Are you crazy?* look.

"Late-night graffiti artist."

She huffed, "You are really obnoxious."

"I've got it. Hot biker babe?"

Not even a smile, though she did roll her eyes.

"I guess I'm wondering what's with all the black."

"And I'm wondering why you think it's any of your business," she said coolly.

I'm not gonna lie. Her refusal to warm up to me kind of dented my ego.

"So, this is a joke, right?" Her brown eyes held no amusement.

"Not a joke." *Unfortunately.*

"Why would you need someone to *pretend* to be your girlfriend? Luke Prescott, spoiled rich kid can't get a girlfriend for real?" Her tone was harsh.

Luke Prescott, spoiled rich kid. She clearly had no idea how offensive that was. But I wasn't about to tell her. It wasn't as if I was a Prescott by choice. Very few people knew how much I hated living under the dark shadow cast by my father. My family's reputation was severely—and deservedly— tarnished because of him. I couldn't wait for college. Couldn't wait to get away from him.

"I don't want a real girlfriend."

"What if I don't like boys?" She arched an eyebrow.

"Seriously?" I hadn't considered that complication. When I'd asked around about her, I hadn't been able to come up with much. No one seemed to know a thing about her past relationships. "Doesn't matter," I decided. "You just have to pretend to like me."

"Pretend. Right."

"So you'll do it?"

She met my gaze. "Hell. No." And she began to slide out of the booth.

"You're lucky you're not eighteen. A pretty girl like you, I don't think you'd do well in jail."

She froze at the edge of her seat. The word "jail" had nailed her in place. Her tough act slipped. I saw real fear in her eyes.

"I'll be seventeen for a while longer," she said quietly.

"I've heard juvie's not much better." The statement sounded harsh, but I couldn't let this girl slip away. She might think I was just messing with her, but the truth was I *needed* her. And if she couldn't deal with the consequences, she shouldn't have been painting the graffiti in the first place.

"You would seriously turn me in?" She looked at me with such disgust I felt my gut twist into a knot.

"Meg, if you would give me a chance, you'll see I'm not such a bad guy." It's not like I wanted to do this. Not really. Lately, almost everything in my life had me feeling like I was backed into a corner. Meg could be my way out.

"Really? 'Cause if that's the case, you can prove it to me right now. You could say, 'Hey, Meg. Remember that thing I saw you doing? Let's forget I tried to blackmail you and let's both go on our merry ways.' Because that," she said, "would definitely make me believe you're a nice guy. This blackmailing? Not so much. So can we forget this happened?"

Her pleading tone made me cringe. "I can't let this go."

"Not can't...won't."

I leaned across the table, and she pushed back in her seat, as if she couldn't stand to be any closer to me. "Why do you have to be so damn stubborn?" I growled.

She stared at me in disbelief. "I'm sorry. Should I thank you for *blackmailing* me?"

"You could *thank* me for not turning you in. Not only would Mr. Prichard like to know, but while I was in his office I heard mention of cooperating with the police." I took a sip of my malt, giving her time to think it over.

"Fine," she said through gritted teeth. "I'll do it."

"Good." I tamped down a sigh of relief. I didn't want her to know that this actually meant a lot to me.

"Are you at least going to tell me why?"

I couldn't blame her for asking. Didn't mean I had to answer. "I don't really think that's any of your business."

"I'd make a better pretend girlfriend if I knew why I was pretending. Are you trying to make Jaclyn jealous?"

The thought made me cringe. "No. I want the opposite, actually. I broke up with her. She's having a hard time accepting it."

Meg motioned for me to go on. I chose my words carefully.

"Her dad works for my dad. Our moms have been friends forever. They've practically been grooming us for marriage since we were in diapers," I explained. "I wouldn't be surprised if those two have started planning our wedding."

"That's kind of disturbing. You're not even out of high school yet." She shrugged. "So date someone else. I'm sure you could find someone who is actually interested in you."

"I don't want someone who is interested in me. I want *you*."

"*Why?*"

"No one in my circle would dare go out with me right now. Jaclyn would make them miserable. Also, I don't want to deal with something as time intensive as a real girlfriend. I have too much going on with baseball and school. Plus, I don't want to lead anyone on. You know?" It was a partial truth, so I didn't feel too bad.

"So it's okay for her to make my life hell?"

"She won't. You know why? Because *you* don't care what she thinks. The other girls do. But that's not really the point of this. What I want is a girl I don't have to get emotionally involved with."

"So don't date anyone."

It sounded like a rational suggestion. But Meg didn't know the whole story. And I wasn't about to tell her.

"As long as Jaclyn thinks I'm single, she won't let up."

"Poor baby."

"Look, she cries to her mommy, who in turn lays it on thick to my mom, who in turn tears me a new one every time I walk into the room. She can't understand why I won't get back together with her. Especially since I'm not seeing anyone else."

The fragment of truth I gave finally looked like it clicked into place. "But if you *were* seeing someone else, you'd have an excuse. Jaclyn wouldn't come on so strong. And your mom wouldn't press you as hard."

"Exactly." I waited, clenching my fists at my sides, wondering if the explanation I gave would be enough for her. It would have to be. There was no way I could tell her everything. She would never understand.

"If this is happening, we need rules," she said.

I relaxed now that her inquisition was over. "Agreed." I tugged a notebook out of my backpack and slapped it down on the table. A pen was crammed into the spiral binding. I pulled it out.

"All right, Meg," I started, keeping my tone light. "What are our rules of persuasion?"

She gave me a blank stare. "Our what?"

"How are we going to persuade everyone that this is real?" I tapped the pen against the paper.

"Those weren't the sort of rules I was talking about. I was thinking more about rules for you," she clarified.

Rules for me? What did *that* mean?

She twirled a lock of that fiery-red hair around her finger. "I don't even know where to begin."

I decided to start simple. "You eat lunch with me."

"No. No way."

"No way?" She looked at me as if I'd asked her to dance on the lunch table. What was so wrong with sitting with me? Did she really think I was that horrible to be around?

"No," she repeated.

I frowned.

"Look." She rested her elbows on the table. "I like eating lunch with my friends. Eating with you? It would be awkward. Besides, I would feel like a cling-on. Think of it this way. If I give you some space, your friends will think better of me for it."

"How so?" I couldn't see where she was going with this.

"I don't want your friends, or mine, to think I'm using you to edge into your snobby inner circle. And I like eating lunch with my friends."

Maybe she had a point. Though I took issue with her use of *snobby*. "Fine. You don't have to eat lunch with me."

"Also, no kissing."

She had to be joking. How could we date without at least a few kisses? Is that what she meant by making rules for me? "That's not gonna fly."

A slightly panicked look landed on her face.

"Hey," I said lightly, "we need to make this believable. I'm not saying we have to have a full-on make-out session at my locker every morning." She shivered. In relief? I tried not to take offense and pushed ahead.

"But if the situation arises, it's going to look suspicious if there isn't at least a little PDA. Like you said, we come from different circles. My friends, and yours, are going to need some persuading. We're going to have to work at selling this."

She blinked at me, those big brown eyes silently pleading.

"Wait." I studied her face and winced as I read her displeasure. "You have been kissed before, right? Like kissing me wouldn't be your first time? 'Cause I could see how you would want a first kiss to mean something. If you've never kissed anyone, I don't want to push you into doing something you don't want to do."

She frowned. "Of course I've been kissed before. But thank you for making me feel like that's so hard to believe."

"I don't find it hard to believe. In fact, I find you *very* kissable." I hoped a bit of flirting would soften her up, cause that tough facade of hers to crumble a bit. "In case no one has told you before, you're really kind of beautiful."

Her mouth dropped open, and she quickly snapped it shut.

"Moving on." She tapped my notebook with a pink fingernail. "No embellishing our relationship."

"Right." I grinned. "No telling them we're planning a trip to Vegas to elope."

She glared at me. "Not funny. You know what I mean."

"I was teasing. You should try lightening up." I tapped the pen against the page and wrote down the next rule. "No embellishing our love life."

"You pay for everything."

"Done." Covering our dates was a small price to pay, considering what I had riding on this, if all went according to my plan.

We spent nearly half an hour squabbling over the specifics of our arrangement. Meg had a knack for fighting me every step of the way. When I requested we spend four evenings a week together, she thought one was plenty. We settled on three. I was insistent she meet my parents at some point. She would have to, for this plan to work. She was adamant that we leave hers out of it. I was determined our friends could never learn of our plan. She argued that she had to tell her friends because they'd never believe she was interested in me. Again...*ouch*. But whatever. If she needed to tell her friends in order for this to work, I really couldn't argue too much.

"Anything else?" I asked.

She looked longingly at her empty malt glass. I was glad I'd ordered her one. At least I'd done something right.

"Nothing I can think of right now." She glanced at my notebook. The first hint of a smile appeared. "You condensed our entire conversation down to two rules? How typical of a guy to cut out the fluff and get to the point."

"Well, yeah. Why bother with...*fluff*?" I didn't see the need to complicate matters.

The rules were simple enough:

Take things slow (her rule)

Make it believable (my rule)

I flipped the notebook shut and wrangled it into my backpack. "I guess we're done here."

"Finally." Her smile evaporated again. "I guess I'll see you later." She slid out of the booth, not waiting for a good-bye.

I yanked a few bills out of my wallet and tossed them on the table to cover the malts with plenty left for a tip. Grabbing my backpack, I darted out of the restaurant.

I didn't need girls to be falling at my feet. But I wasn't used to them acting as if I wasn't worth their time. Meg's indifference rattled me. As I watched her head to her Rebel—as if she couldn't get away from me fast enough—I felt the urge to rattle her right back.

"Meg!"

She twisted around slowly.

I sauntered up to her until there were only inches between us. To her credit, she didn't back down.

"I thought we were done," she said. Was it my imagination, or did she sound slightly breathless?

"Not quite."

She cleared her throat and took a step back. I reached for her hands, tangling my fingers around hers as I reeled her back in. "We forgot to seal the deal."

"Seal the deal?"

"Seal it with a kiss." I shrugged. "You're going to have to kiss me eventually. Personally, I'd rather have our first time be without an audience. Wouldn't you?"

She winced, clearly knowing that I was right.

"I guess it would be best to get the awkwardness out of the way," she grumbled.

I decided not to focus on the fact that she sounded less than thrilled. Instead, I took it as a good sign that she didn't elbow me in the gut and storm away.

I moved in slowly, not convinced she wouldn't bolt. Her eyes fluttered closed. Her hands slid up my arms, clutching at my biceps. When her lips met mine I swear something ignited between us. My hands gripped her waist and as the kiss lingered, the tension melted away.

She had acted so cold toward me, the last thing I expected was for the kiss to be so hot.

Chapter Four

Stupid boy.

His kiss tasted like chocolate.

Stupid *me* for enjoying it. Even worse? I couldn't stop thinking about it. The kiss should've felt forced but it hadn't. It had taken some effort on my part to pull away. Then, I just stood there, embarrassingly breathless as I held onto Luke for support. I thought he would gloat, but he looked as surprised as I felt. Eventually I regained my senses, but the damage had been done. The kiss was permanently etched into my memory.

After meeting with Luke, I'd gone for a jog through the park at the edge of town. Unlike most days, it did little to calm me.

"I've gotten myself into such a mess," I told Lady as I finished brushing out my shower dampened hair.

She was flopped on her side at the foot of my bed, too tired from our run to give me much notice. Her stubby tail gave a half-hearted wiggle. I plopped down on the edge of my bed, scratching behind her ears.

Mom had read an article about the healing power of pet companions. Within the week she had scoured every animal shelter in a hundred-mile radius. She'd found Lady, a surrendered cocker spaniel whose original owner had gone into a nursing home.

For the last few months of her life, Sydney had barely been able to get out of bed. Her damaged heart couldn't handle the strain. Lady had been a comfort to her. It was hard to look at the dog now and not think of my sister.

I would never forget the countless number of days I'd curled up in bed next to her as we watched classic movies. Or the days I'd spent studying my homework while she doodled in her ever-present sketchpad. I nudged the memory away when I felt my eyes begin to burn.

Now that Sydney was gone, Lady had become my responsibility. I didn't mind.

What I *did* mind was Luke's nosiness.

What right did he have to ask me about the clothes I wore? Only my best friends had realized I'd started wearing black the day of Sydney's funeral and simply never stopped. Francesca thought it was morbid. But I knew there were cultures who wore black for years to show they were in mourning after a death. I didn't find it that odd. But that was something I would never share with *him*.

I glanced around my room. Sydney's drawings were dotted all over my sloping walls. The pictures were like having a little piece of my sister with me. Feeling her presence calmed me, made me feel closer to her.

After Sydney got sick, Mom decided to quit her job to care for her. Between the loss of her paycheck and the addition of Sydney's medical expenses, my parents felt their only choice was to downsize.

I never minded. If a terminal illness was good for one

thing, it was readjusting a person's priorities.

Now we lived in a small, antiquated house a few blocks from downtown. Our neighbors were so close that it was easy to unintentionally eavesdrop if windows were left open. Sydney had been given the only bedroom on the ground floor. Climbing stairs had been too taxing on her body. My parents and I had rooms at the top of a narrow staircase. Our rooms were cut short by the slanted ceiling of the low roof. My bedroom in this house was barely bigger than my walk-in closet in our old house. But we had been happy enough.

Or we had been in the beginning, when Sydney had been doing okay. When she started to slip, everything changed.

Now happy and normal were distant memories.

During my run, I'd realized hopping onto Luke's blackmail bandwagon really was in my best interest. The last thing my parents needed was to find out their remaining child was a criminal.

Dad was stressed enough having to deal with Mom.

As for Mom, she wasn't even able to cope with life as it was.

I was reminded of this yet again as I tiptoed down the staircase.

The pleading tone in Dad's voice made me cringe. "Marion, you have got to snap out of this. You need to get out of the house. Go to lunch with your friends. Get a massage. Hell, meet with a therapist. Just do *something*."

His plea was met by silence.

"You are not the only one who lost a daughter. Why can't you understand that?"

"I'm sorry, Rick. Today was hard." Mom sounded worn, beaten. As if she didn't have any emotion left to give.

"I'm sure it was." Dad sounded just as beaten. "My day wasn't so great, either. I had a general contractor try to back out of an order. Problem was, I'd already mixed the forty-five gallons of paint he'd ordered for a new hotel he's working on. I had to threaten to take him to court. I've been working fifty, sixty hour weeks. The medical bills are rolling in, and I don't know how we'll ever pay them all." He sighed. "I'm struggling, too. When I come home after a ten-hour day, is it too much to hope that we could sit down and have a conversation? Is it too much to ask that we have a meal together?"

"You just…" She paused a moment to find the right words. "You don't understand. I put everything into caring for Sydney. *Everything*. I feel like I don't have anything left to give right now."

"And I didn't help care for her?" Dad's tone was careful, measured.

"Not the way I did. I was with her night and day. I never left her side," Mom said. "Now that she's gone, I feel like a piece of me has been ripped away."

I bit my lip and thought the words Dad spoke aloud. "And you don't think Meg and I feel that way, too?"

I edged into the kitchen.

Mom tried to tug a hand through her auburn hair. It was a tangled mess, and she quickly gave up. "You don't understand."

Dad blew out a frustrated breath. Those words seemed to be her mantra.

I had walked in on conversations similar to this countless times. No matter how many times it happened, I would never get used to the helpless way it made me feel. I offered the only distraction I could think of. "I'll make dinner."

"Meg." Dad grimaced as he finally focused on me. "I didn't realize you were home."

I moved to the fridge, sending up a silent prayer that I could find something to throw together. Half the battle of cooking dinner was finding something to make. The fridge and cupboards were pretty bare these days because Mom avoided shopping.

"No, there's nothing in the cupboards anyway. We'll go out." Dad turned to me. "What are you hungry for?"

"Anything."

"If I never eat another bite of pizza in my life," Dad grumbled, "I would be okay with that."

Having a pizza delivered had become our go-to method of making dinner. In the beginning we had ordered the standard pepperoni, maybe an occasional sausage. As the months dragged by we'd switched it up to Hawaiian, Mexican, chicken Alfredo. But pizza was still pizza, and it all got old after a while.

Fifteen minutes later, Dad and I parked in front of Maebelle's. The familiar vinyl lettering in the window proclaimed "old fashioned home cooking." It was why Dad usually chose this place.

I dropped into a booth toward the back. This table was on the opposite side from where Luke and I sat only hours earlier. Thankfully, a new set of waitresses was on duty.

The small changes made me feel better. I didn't want to have to explain that awkwardness.

After our meals were ordered—a meatloaf dinner for Dad, lasagna for me—Dad seemed to deflate in front of my eyes.

"Look, Meg, I'm sorry you had to hear all of that."

"It's fine."

He shook his head. I realized then how much he'd aged in the past year. How had I not noticed it before? His dark hair was thinner, grayer. Deep lines bracketed the edges of his brown eyes. He didn't look as weary as Mom, but he sure didn't look good.

"No, it's not fine," he corrected. "I'm at a point where I don't know what to do anymore. Your mother seems to be getting worse rather than better. I'm worried about her. That's

why something has got to change. I've given her space. I've
coddled her. I've let her fill up on those damn anti-depressants.
I've tried everything I can think of to get her through this. The
only thing I haven't tried is a hefty dose of tough love. And
frankly," he said on a weary sigh, "tough love is about the only
type of love I have left for her right now."

"What are you saying?"

"I'm saying *I* can't go on like this." He scraped his hands
over his face.

"So, you're abandoning her?" I tried to keep the edge of
accusation out of my tone. On a deeper level, I understood
where he was coming from. But on an emotional level, I didn't
understand it at all. Our family was already broken. Why was
he determined to shatter it completely?

My appetite had faded into an aching hollowness.

Dad looked hurt. "I'm not abandoning her. I'm trying to
give her a reason to want to change. I'm burning myself right
out and sometimes, I'm not even sure why. It's not as if your
mother appreciates it."

My jaw reflexively clenched, and I had to look away from
him.

"Before you judge me, you have no idea how much it
pains me to say that. I lost a daughter the same day she did. I
also lost my wife that day. I want her back."

His voice cracked, and now he was the one looking away.
He blinked hard, and the shimmer in his eyes did not go
unnoticed by me.

"If you can think of another way to make that happen,
tell me now," he said.

I had no answers for him.

"I want you to know that if I move out, I have every
intention of taking you with me."

"Move out?" My voice was edged with panic.

"Yes," he said quietly. "It's been on my mind for some

time now. I'm so sorry it's come to this, but I'm at my wits' end."

Our waitress appeared with two steaming plates. Her presence saved me from having to come up with a response. I was grateful because really, what could I possibly say?

. . .

I had texted Francesca and Kylie before school asking them to meet me in the parking lot. Luke had also been waiting. He grinned when he saw me, and then frowned as I darted into Francesca's vehicle. Our imaginary romance was not getting off to a stellar start. Feeling inexplicably guilty, I had tossed him what I hoped was a flirtatious smile and wave before nearly yanking Francesca's door off the hinges.

Now, less than five minutes later, I had caught them up on the melodrama that had become my life. Or at least the melodrama regarding Luke. I couldn't bring myself to talk about my parents this morning. They said nothing during my entire monologue. Now they stared at me as if a stranger had tumbled into the front seat.

Francesca shook her head with a scowl. "Luke Prescott in a *fake* relationship."

Kylie pinched the bridge of her nose as she poked her head between the seats. "I'm sorry…I'm still stuck on the fact that *you're* the one that painted the school."

"What am I going to do?" I lamented.

"Sounds like you have no choice other than to go along with it." Francesca's tone was matter-of-fact.

"My head is still spinning," Kylie said, "but we better go or we'll be late."

She was right. The parking lot had emptied out. Luke was gone. Knowing this made it easier to crawl out of the security of Francesca's vehicle.

My feeling of relief was short-lived.

Luke was resting against my locker. He was tapping away on his phone. A moment later my cell vibrated in my back pocket. It didn't matter that I chose to ignore it. I could ignore my phone, but I couldn't ignore him. He felt the weight of my gaze. His eyes met mine across the sea of people.

He did not look happy. And an unhappy Luke, I knew, had the potential to lead to an incarcerated Meg.

I had to do some damage control.

I swerved my way through the crowd as I squeezed a smile onto my face.

"Luke," I said softly, "I didn't know you'd be waiting for me." I wanted to tack on *It wasn't covered in the rules.*

"Why wouldn't I be?" He moved toward me and tossed his arm around my shoulders. "It would've been nice of you to at least say hi this morning." There was an edge to his tone, warning me I had better make time for him tomorrow morning. "Meet me in the parking lot after school?"

I agreed, and he released me. I felt oddly pleased that his tone implied it was a request, not a command.

"Good. See you then." He gave my shoulder a final squeeze before disappearing into the crowd.

By lunchtime the school was buzzing with news that made my knees quake.

"Did you hear there's a reward?" Francesca leaned across our lunch table. "I heard Mrs. Dahlberg talking to Mr. Thomas. So far the Parent Teacher Association has put together a thousand dollars for any information leading to the vandal."

"I really messed up," I said in a low voice.

She scowled. "Do you think he'll tell?"

I shot a quick glance toward Luke's table. He was listening to his friends' banter as he attacked his cheeseburger. He didn't look my way, and I quickly returned my attention to Francesca.

I shook my head. "No. It's not like he needs the money. He really wants to play out this dating charade. I think it means more to him than a thousand dollars ever would."

"So as long as you do what he says, your secret is safe."

Was a single hour going to pass by when I was not reminded of the enormous hole I'd dug myself into?

Francesca leaned back in her seat. Her smile turned mischievous. "You're lucky I'm such a good friend. I could sure use a thousand bucks."

My eyebrows puckered together. "That's not funny."

Her grin broadened. "It's at least a little bit funny."

Chapter Five

Jaclyn was the first person I spotted staring us down as we walked out of school together holding hands. I hadn't trusted Meg to make it out to the parking lot without a chaperone. Her twitchy behavior throughout the day had me convinced she'd bolt. I was there the moment she slammed her locker door shut.

"Jaclyn definitely noticed us," I said, more to myself than Meg.

"What? No gloating?" she scoffed as we pulled out of the lot. "I thought you'd want to rub it in her face that you're supposedly seeing someone else."

I shot her an irritated look. "Thanks for thinking so highly of me."

"Are we just going to wait until the parking lot clears out before you bring me back?"

"Actually, I thought we could drive around for a while."

She frowned. "Why?"

It grated on me knowing that this girl seemed determined to hate every second she had to spend with me. I didn't want her to, like, *love* me. But it bothered me more than I would care to admit that she didn't even *like* me.

I was determined to change that.

"If we're going to pretend to be dating, we need to get to know one another. I can't be dating a girl and not know a damn thing about her."

She slumped down in her seat. I didn't give her a chance to argue.

"Where do you live?"

"I'm not involving my parents in this," she warned. "There's no reason for you to know where I live."

"I can't date a girl and not know where she lives."

This was met by a moment of silence. I braced myself for another argument. Despite the kiss I couldn't stop thinking about, I was wondering if this whole situation was going to be worth the trouble Meg could certainly bring.

"Cherry Lane. I had better not see you there." She narrowed her eyes at me and then whipped around, dangling off the arm rest as she dug for something behind us.

"Did you just unzip my backpack?" I was more amused than irritated.

She flopped back down in the passenger seat. A lock of hair floated in front of her face. With a puff, she blew it out of the way.

My ratty green notebook was clenched in her hand. She flipped until she found the page she was looking for, and then pulled a hot pink pen out of her purse.

She verbalized her command as she scribbled it across the page.

Luke cannot go to Meg's house. Ever.

"Bossy, aren't you?"

"Me? You're mad I spent the morning with Francesca and Kylie." The pen flew across the page again. Never mind that I was driving, she held it up for me to see. "Does this rule fit your requirements?"

Meg must devote every morning to Luke.

"It's perfect." I grinned, refusing to be baited by her sarcasm. "You have lunch with your friends. Mornings should be mine." I craned my neck. "What else are you writing?"

"I'm playing catch-up because your rules are severely lacking. This," she said, "is for last night."

Luke cannot kiss Meg whenever he wants.

I chuckled. "Okay. Kiss only as needed. Kinda like taking an aspirin."

She gave me the evil eye before saying, "Where are we headed?"

"Nowhere in particular, just thought we could drive around."

"Sounds spectacular."

"Do you want anything? I could get you a latte? A chocolate malt? Green smoothie?"

"I'm good."

We drove in silence for a few minutes as I navigated the downtown traffic.

"So what's our story?" she demanded. "How did we end up together?"

I tossed around some scenarios in my head. "Okay. Got it. You and your Rebel caught my interest. I asked around to see if you had a boyfriend. When I found out you didn't, I asked if you'd be willing to meet me at Maebelle's. You agreed. It fits perfectly with our meeting last night. We started talking, found out we had a lot in common." I glanced at her to see if she approved so far. She nodded and I continued. "We left Maebelle's and went for a drive. Before the night was over, I asked you out. This relationship is just starting, but it's going to get serious fast."

She made a noncommittal sound. "What could we possibly have in common?"

I reached over and squeezed her knee. "Come on, babe, we can figure something out."

"First of all," she slid my hand away, "do not call me babe."

The irritation in her voice surprised me. "Why not?"

"It's tacky."

"How is it tacky?"

"What did you call Jaclyn?"

"Babe."

"What about the girls before her?"

"Babe." I winced. It was possible this little spitfire had a point.

"See? Tacky. You are not going to add me to a long string of 'babes.' It's demeaning. I mean, could you possibly use a more generic nickname?"

"Right," I agreed, proud of myself for seeing her point of view. "Because you, *you* need to stand out."

"That's not what I meant."

"You need a nickname all your own." I liked the idea, myself.

"Not really. I don't—"

"I'll work on it." I tossed her a reassuring wink.

"Fabulous."

"What sports do you like?" I asked.

She hesitated. "I hate sports. All sports."

"Even baseball?"

"Even baseball," she confirmed.

"That's too bad. I live for baseball. I've been throwing the ball around since I was a toddler."

"Well, then, you're lucky you get to play, aren't you?" she asked. "Not everyone is given that chance."

"Yeah, well, if my dad has anything to say about it, I won't be playing for long," I admitted. "He thinks baseball is a waste of time. He stopped coming to my games after Little League. As soon as my high school career is over he expects me to drop the game."

I glanced at her. She quirked an eyebrow as if to ask, *Why should I care?*

Less than twenty-four hours in and I realized fake-dating might be more exhausting than dating for real.

I tried again. "What *do* you like?"

"Spending time with my friends."

"That's not very helpful." I thought for a moment. "Do you surf?" Surfing wasn't great around here but an hour or so down the coast it wasn't too bad.

"No. Do you?"

"Not anymore, but I'd resurrect my interest if it would help our cause."

We were headed out of town on a southbound road. I knew we had to have something in common. I also realized that Meg was not likely to help me figure out what that something was. When she started to fidget, tapping her hands on her thighs, I gave her a questioning look.

"You're right. We should be able to think of something," she said.

"Okay?" Her sudden agreeableness was confusing.

"Movies? Books? Music? What do you like?"

"This is why I thought it would be a good idea to go for a drive. We can talk. Figure this out."

"Uh-huh." Her tapping became more intense. She squirmed in her seat. "You know what? I'm hungry after all. I'm actually *starving*. Can we head back to town?"

"Now?" I had dated some confusing girls, but Meg was

starting to top the charts. "You weren't hungry ten minutes ago."

"I was nervous ten minutes ago. Slow down." She pointed to a splotch of gravel that spread off from the road we were traveling down. "You can turn around there."

I didn't slow down. "What is with you?"

I could almost feel Meg's anxiety hanging in the cab of my Navigator. The look she wore was awfully close to panic. Was she suddenly afraid of me?

"Turn around," she begged.

"Okay, fine," I agreed. "I'll turn at the next approach. There's one right after the overpass."

We coasted past the cement supports that bookended each side of the road, hoisting the overpass into the air. The supports were made of wide expanses of cement block. They made a perfect canvas. Apparently they made an *irresistible* canvas.

"What the hell," I muttered. I had driven under this overpass dozens of times. I might have even spotted the mural before. The difference was, until a few nights ago I had no idea who this artwork belonged to.

No wonder she wanted me to turn around.

She closed her eyes and blew out a strained sigh.

"You little criminal."

"Shut up." It wasn't a great comeback, but she went with it.

"*You*…you are something else." Laughter rolled out of my mouth.

"Stop talking."

"Oh, Meg. You have been a busy, busy girl," I teased.

"I hate you. Do you know that? I really, really do."

"Nah," I disagreed. "I don't think so. I think you're mad at yourself right now. You're just taking it out on me."

"So," she said flatly. "Movies? Books? Music? What do

you like?"

"Back to that?" I wasn't stupid. "You wouldn't be trying to keep me from asking how much painting you've been doing, would you?"

She tossed her hands in the air. "That's it. Those are the only two."

My words were slow, deliberate, amused. "You little liar."

"I'm not lying. I've just painted the two. I guess you must be super lucky. You've seen them both."

"I'm lucky all right." I didn't even try to shake the smug grin I wore. "Do you always create the same design? Makes it pretty easy to spot." The heart with detailed angel wings sprouting from it was identical to the mural on the school.

"Yes, always," she said. "You've proven your point. You have dirt on me. You practically own me. For now, I am your puppet."

My laughter faded. She sounded so dejected. "Aw, come on. Don't be so pissy about this."

"Don't be pissy? Under the circumstances is there any other way for me to be?"

"Let's talk about music," I suggested, hoping to bring us back to safer emotional ground.

"Good idea."

By the time we headed back to town we had decided on movies and music we could both get by with pretending to have a common interest in. It was enough. I knew my friends would never question it. Meg was gorgeous, and that would be enough of an explanation for them. My parents and Jaclyn might need some convincing.

"One of these nights I think you should come over for a study date." I watched her, trying to gauge her reaction.

"To your house?" She sounded incredulous.

"It'll have to be, since you made it clear your house is off-limits. Right?"

"Right," she confirmed. "I'm not sure I'm ready to meet your parents yet. I need to ease my way into this. Meeting parents, and answering questions, that's more like a full-on submersion."

"I'll pick a night when they aren't home."

"Can't we just pretend to have a study date?"

"No," I argued. "My friends usually stop by. You need to be there. Besides, I still don't feel like I know you very well. Where's the notebook?"

We were back in town, a few blocks from the school. I zipped over to the side of the road, parking in front of an old Victorian.

I reached across her, grabbing the notebook off the dash. I plucked the funky pink pen out of her hand—where she'd been twirling it between her fingers.

Meg will stop being difficult and will cooperate with Luke.

"Fine." Her face crinkled in thought. "I love hot chocolate. I don't drink coffee. It smells bad and reminds me of waiting rooms. My favorite way to spend a rainy day is curled up with a blanket watching black and white movies. I have a black cocker spaniel named Lady. I think fish are stupid pets. What's the point? They just die on you. At the risk of sounding like a cliché, I love pink." She stopped talking and raised an eyebrow. "Are we good now? Is that cooperative enough? I don't know what else to tell you. I'm actually pretty boring."

"You are not boring. You *are* uptight, though." My words earned me a death glare. "Loosen up. We should try to have some fun with this."

I tossed the notebook back up on the dash. Her feet tapped restlessly against the floor as we cruised down the street again. Either the girl had a lot of nervous energy, or she was still anxious to get away from me.

The lot was mostly deserted now as I pulled up next to Meg's Rebel.

She twisted around again, this time reaching for her bag.

"You've got to be kidding me."

"What?" I craned my neck to look as well.

She motioned to the box full of baseball bats. They all still had price stickers stuck to them.

"I'm not sure how I missed those before, but seriously?" she asked. "Is that really necessary? I mean, I'm not a baseball expert but how many bats does one boy need?"

It would've been easy to explain to Meg what the bats were for. But her obvious disgust had me feeling defensive. "That's also not any of your business."

"Whatever." She tugged her bag onto her lap and reached for the door handle.

I grabbed her wrist. "One more thing."

She turned to me and raised an eyebrow.

"There's something I forgot to mention." It was a piece pivotal to my plan.

"And what," she asked feigning indifference, "would that be?"

"When the time comes, I'm the one who ends things."

"Of course you will." She rolled her eyes. "Fine. But can I at least request that it's done respectfully? Like, don't cheat on me? Don't trash me? That kind of thing."

"You have my word," I promised.

She shoved the door open and hopped out.

"Tonight was a good start, letting everyone see us leave together. But I expect you to step up your game, Meg. Make them believe it," I ordered.

Hearing the veiled threat, she nodded before slamming the door.

Chapter Six

MEG

The next morning, acting like a dutiful girlfriend, I made my way over to Luke after parking in the back of the lot. My helmet was safely tucked into my hard-sided saddle bag. I fidgeted with my hair as I walked, fingering my way through a few wayward tangles.

I realized people were staring. My initial instinct was to scamper into the school. Luckily my survival instinct kicked in. I realized I could make this moment work for me.

My boots slapped against the pavement.

My heart slammed against my chest.

My fingernails dug into my palms.

Luke was standing with his best friend, Adam, and a few other guys I recognized. Though he wore aviators to fight off the brilliance of the morning sun, I could feel him watching me.

I strode across the parking lot with an inflated sense of purpose. Luke gave me a subtle nod of approval.

"Hey, there," I cooed in my sassiest, most playful voice. Though it probably wasn't sassy at all. I probably sounded ridiculous. I pressed a quick kiss to his cheek. He had wanted me to up my game. Did this count?

"Well, hello, Nutmeg." He pulled me into a bear hug, gripping me so tightly that he pulled me onto my tiptoes. A shorter girl would've been left dangling. My chin slid over his shoulder and I found myself looking straight into Jaclyn's eyes. Her expression remained carefully impassive, except for the slight twitching of an eyebrow. I quickly looked away. While Jaclyn was no friend of mine, I certainly didn't want to make her an enemy.

He dropped me onto my feet again but pulled me close.

"Nutmeg?" Jaclyn snickered.

"Nutmeg," he repeated. He reached up and twisted a lock of my hair around his finger. "The color of her hair? It's freaking gorgeous. And she doesn't even need to go to a salon to get it."

Jaclyn's eyes narrowed. Her fingers trembled, as if she were about to run a hand over her own very chemically produced hair color with its multitude of blond highlights and lowlights.

"Nutmeg," I echoed. I'd always thought my hair was the color of cinnamon…but nutmeg was a good descriptor, too.

I tossed the nickname around in my head and mentally rolled my eyes. *Nutmeg.*

He let go of the curl he'd formed. His eyes never left mine as he winked and said, "I guess I could call you Red, but that's so…*generic.*"

An honest to goodness giggle slipped out. I slapped my hand over my mouth, as if I could take it back. Luke grinned at me. Not his cocky grin, but one that looked genuinely pleased.

"You like it?"

"It'll do," I said airily.

"So, Meg, I'm Adam." Of course I knew who he was, but we'd never actually had a conversation. "Luke's told me a lot about you."

I sliced a curious glance at Luke. "Really?"

"I haven't said much." He gave my shoulder a reassuring squeeze, presumably to let me know my secret was safe. "Adam's the Wildcats' catcher."

Luke's tone cued me in to the fact that this was supposed to be important.

I smiled at Adam. "That's awesome."

"You ever watch us play?" Adam asked.

I contemplated a fib, but decided on the truth. "No."

"But you will this season. Right?" Luke asked.

The upcoming season was months away. Regardless, I gave him the answer I knew he wanted. "Absolutely."

Jaclyn, who had been standing to the side with Meredith and Bethany, snorted as she rolled her eyes. Her disdain could've been aimed at any number of things. The way Luke was holding me close. The idea that I would still be around come next spring. The silly, but sort of sweet, nickname Luke had given me. Overall, I thought her scorn was aimed at my very existence.

"We better head inside." Without another word, the trio spun on their collective chunky heels and sashayed away.

"We should go, too," Luke announced.

"I need to find Trevor," Adam said. He started walking backward, pointing a finger at Luke. "You'll talk to Meg about later?"

"Yeah," Luke said. "See you around."

Adam twisted and took off at a jog.

"Talk to me about what?"

"Do you work tonight?"

While arguing about how much time we needed to spend

together I had mentioned I worked for my dad.

"No. Why?"

"We're going to meet Adam and the others for pizza." I frowned at his bossiness. "Please?" he amended.

"I don't know."

"Why not?"

I didn't like pizza, and I didn't like the thought of spending time with his friends. I went with the less volatile excuse. "I don't like pizza."

"Seriously? How can you not like pizza?" He shook his head. "I don't know if I can even date someone who doesn't like pizza. That's just wrong." I brightened at this and he laughed. "You're not getting out of it that easily. They have other things on the menu. Order pasta or something."

"And stand out like some freak who doesn't like pizza? No, thanks."

"Just trying to help." His arm slid away from my shoulders once we were inside the school. He paused before heading toward the hallway that led to his locker. "After school. Don't forget."

As if I could.

• • •

At the end of the day, before I'd even tucked my books away, Luke was at my locker.

"Just in case you were planning on trying to escape," he said.

"The thought never crossed my mind."

This was our first time out with his friends. Thoughts of escaping had hijacked my brain all day.

"Liar."

He escorted me to his SUV. I stopped to chat with Francesca and Kylie along the way, prolonging the inevitable.

Eventually Luke tugged me away.

"You should reconsider letting me drive you to school." Luke tapped his hands on the steering wheel as he drove.

He had insisted I ride with him on our way to meet his friends. I wasn't going to let him bully me into being my permanent chauffer.

"We've been over this. My parents"—*my dad*, I silently corrected—"would want to know who you are."

"Tell them I'm your friend," he suggested.

"I am not lying to my parents on account of you."

His tone softened. "Meg, you don't have to lie. We can be friends, can't we?"

"I don't think so." It seemed intrinsically wrong to befriend the person who insisted on holding your puppet strings. "Does it really matter whether or not you drive me to school?"

"I feel like I should. It's the proper thing to do."

"I like riding my motorcycle." It was true.

"I could see why. I guess if you have to drive yourself, that's the way to go." He contemplated that. "Actually, it's fine if you want to drive yourself. The guys all think your Rebel is smokin.'"

"The guys talk about me?"

He gave me a confounded look. "Well, yeah. You are my girlfriend. You're hot. You ride a bike. Of course they've been talking about you the past few days."

"What do they say?" My tone was slightly panicked.

"That you're hot. And they like your bike," he deadpanned.

I slapped his shoulder. "Don't mock me. What do they say about me?"

"Nothing bad, if that's what you're worried about. They wouldn't dare," he said. "Besides, what could they possibly say that was bad?"

"I don't like people talking about me," I admitted. "No

matter what they say. It's…weird."

Luke angled into a parking spot. I sat motionless, even after he'd shoved the keys into his pocket. I could feel him staring at me.

"Coming?"

I turned to him with a grimace.

"It'll be fine," he said. "You have nothing to be nervous about."

"Am I that obvious?"

He laughed. "You are."

"It's not like I don't have good reason. What if I say something to mess everything up?"

He gave my shoulder a friendly nudge. "That won't happen. I won't let it. It's not like I'm tossing you to a pack of wolves. These are my friends. Besides, I'll be there with you."

Once we were inside, my nervousness began to fade. Adam was there with his girlfriend, Julia. She gave me a cautious smile and a finger wave as Luke pulled out a chair for me. We were met with a flurry of greetings from the rest of his friends. Adam nodded a hello while Leo eyed me with curiosity. Trevor eyed me with something much more blatant.

"Hi," I offered to the group as a whole.

"Glad you could make it," Julia said. She even sounded like she meant it. "I was hoping I wouldn't be the only girl today."

I slid into my chair, and Luke dropped into the one next to me.

"Of course she could make it," he said lightly. "She wants to get to know everyone."

"What can I get the two of you to drink?"

I swung around to look at the waitress who had appeared. Until that moment I hadn't realized the rest of the group already had their drinks.

"Root beer, please," I said.

"I'll have the same," Luke tacked on.

She scanned over the rest of the table. "Are you ready to order, or do you still need a few more minutes?"

"I think we're good to go," Adam decided. He rattled off our table's order, which consisted of three varieties of extra large pizza pies. Our waitress was about to walk away when Luke stopped her.

"We'll take two of the appetizer platters, too."

"Got it," she chirped back at him.

"I can't believe you've never been to a baseball game," Adam chided.

"I guess I've never had a reason to go," I said.

He frowned and shook his head. "It's the best game there is. Our team is awesome. What more reason do you need?"

Julia laughed as she bumped Adam's shoulder with her own. "Give it up. Not everyone loves baseball."

"Well, they should," he grumbled. It was hard to tell if he was joking, or really put out by my lack of love for his sport of choice.

"I might not waste my time at ballgames, either," Trevor said. "Not if I had a bike like that. I'd spend all my time cruising around town. You give out rides on that thing?"

"She doesn't," Luke answered before I could.

"I'm sure she could make an exception," Trevor pressed.

"Not for you, she can't." In another time or place I might be annoyed that Luke was speaking for me. But here and now, I felt grateful.

"If I ever make an exception for anyone, it'll be Luke."

Even though it was a fib, it was the right thing to say. Luke smirked at Trevor.

"Lucky bastard," Trevor mumbled good-naturedly.

"You know who else is lucky?" Adam started. "Whoever had the balls to paint the school the other night. They were damn lucky they didn't get caught."

"Someone will turn them in," Leo said.

My heart skipped a few beats before taking off at a gallop. I slid my hands onto my lap to hide the tremor rumbling through them.

"Nah," Luke said as he grabbed my fingers and squeezed. "If anyone knew anything, they'd have said something by now. They'd want the reward. Whoever did it is in the clear."

Our waitress came back to deposit our drinks. The moment she stepped away I took a sip. I was desperate for any type of distraction.

Leo told the guys he was thinking of getting a new truck, and in seconds their attention was trained on him.

"So, Meg," Julia started, "have you finished reading *The Catcher in the Rye* yet?"

Julia and I were in the same American Lit class. It was *not* an AP English class as Luke loved to point out. I had started the book. But I hadn't had a chance to finish it yet. "Not quite."

She rolled her eyes. "I finished last night. I don't understand how it became an American classic. The writing style is so…dry. And the plot is just…is there a plot? It's so dull it's hard to tell. I mean, it starts off dull, and it doesn't get any better from there."

"You didn't like the book," I surmised.

"It's dull?" Luke interrupted. "Maybe you're interpreting it the wrong way."

He'd clearly foregone the conversation the guys were having to eavesdrop on ours.

"Maybe?" Julia offered.

He frowned before turning back to his friends.

For the next several minutes Julia lamented over the unfairness of the paper we had to write.

When she sat up a little straighter, I realized the waitress had returned with our food. She settled the pizzas on the table first and brought us the appetizer platters on her return trip.

When they arrived, Luke slid one platter to the center of the table for everyone to share. The other platter he slid between us, winking as he nudged it closer to me.

"You do like fried food, right?" He suddenly looked concerned. "Maybe I should've gotten a veggie platter?"

"There are lots of veggie options here." I filled my plate with jalapeno poppers, breaded mushrooms, and onion rings.

I had just stuffed a breaded mushroom in my mouth when Luke's free hand landed on my thigh. It landed just low enough not to be scandalous. His index finger began strumming along the edges of my inseam. He seemed unaware of what he was doing, absently setting my skin ablaze as he picked out a mozzarella stick.

I grabbed his hand under the table and squeezed. A silent warning. He turned to me with a sheepish smile. He probably thought he'd crossed some unwritten line. I hoped he had no idea I needed him to stop because he was making my insides fizz like a can of shaken soda.

Julia jumped back into the conversation, pulling me along with her. But the memory of his fingers skimming my thigh lingered for far longer than I liked.

Chapter Seven

LUKE

"Tell me about this girl," Gabe ordered.

I squeezed my phone in one hand, the steering wheel in the other. Our house was crawling with snobby ladies putting together a charity event for those less privileged than themselves. In their world, that meant just about everyone. When it was over, they'd toast over martinis and pat themselves on the back for helping the people they'd mock on any other given day.

"What do you want to know?" I asked my brother.

"Where did you find her? Does she really ride a motorcycle? Mom said she's one of those Goth chicks. I didn't realize Mom even knew what Goth meant."

"I met her at school. She does ride a Rebel but she's not a Goth chick." I wasn't going to tackle that one.

"She must be amazing if Mom and Dad dislike her so much."

"They don't know her."

Gabe scoffed. "When has that ever mattered? You can probably thank your ex for that. Do you know Mom and Jaclyn have been having lunch together on the weekends? Dad was talking about it at the office."

I bristled, gripping the steering wheel tighter. "I didn't. That would explain a lot though. I knew Mom and Dad wouldn't like Meg. They haven't even met her. But that hasn't stopped them from ripping on her every chance they get."

Mom, especially, was "troubled" by what she hoped was "a simple act of rebellion" and she had faith I'd "come to my senses sooner rather than later."

"No doubt Jaclyn is still pissed that you dumped her, even if it was her fault. She seems like the vindictive type. I'm glad you're rid of her." He chuckled. "From what I've heard, this Meg is the complete opposite of Jaclyn. Dad says it like it's a bad thing. I say hold on to her."

"Gabe. We haven't been together that long." I turned into the city park and cruised to a parking spot closest to the ball field.

"I've got just one piece of advice for you, little brother." Gabe's tone was suddenly serious. "I know it's a long way off, but when you get married, marry for love. That's the one thing I did right in my life. Beth and Madeline make everything else bearable."

"Is it really that bad? Working for Dad?" I rested my head against the seat and waited for the answer I knew was coming. Gabe had been warning me about what was in store for me for a while now.

"Worse. He's got me working on a case right now that curdles my blood. A big corporation is accused of dumping contaminants into a river. Downstream dozens of kids have gotten sick. Two have died. The company refuses to acknowledge any wrongdoing, though everyone knows they're lying. My job is to convince the jury of their innocence." His tone dropped. "I think this billion-dollar corporation has the judge in their pockets. I wish I could find a way to prove it and really bring this little town some justice."

"Would you?" I sat up straight again.

"I would," he finally admitted. "I've been thinking long and hard about this. There's a good chance the other side might be receiving some pertinent information, absolute proof that these chemicals were dumped. It will all be sent anonymously, of course. It would most definitely swing things in their favor."

"You're planning on throwing the case? Dad would disown you if he ever found out."

"He's a pretty shoddy father, but he's a damn good lawyer. He's sneaky, underhanded, *ruthless*. It's not something to brag about, but I've learned a lot from him. He *won't* find out. Once this case is done, so am I. I'm giving up the house, the paycheck, the *guilt*. He always holds my inheritance over my head. I just don't care anymore. Let the bastard write me out of his will. Beth and I are going to start over. I'm thinking some small town, some boring job, a few more kids."

"Damn. I'm impressed." Walking away from Edward Prescott would be a ballsy move.

"Yeah, well. I haven't gone through with it yet." He paused. "Anything new with you? Any luck on the camp in Colorado?"

"What do you think?" I grumbled.

"I think Dad's a jackass. I wish I could just write you a check so you could go."

"It's not about the money," I reminded him. "I'm still a minor. I need a parent's signature."

"Keep working on it. I know what this means to you."

"I'm trying." He knew how important the training camp was—and why—but he had no idea the lengths I was willing to go to try to get there.

He was silent for a moment before saying, "I know I've said this before, but it's worth repeating: Get out from under Dad while you still can. Get out before you're in so deep that you have to claw your way out. Catch you later, kid."

I tossed my phone into the cup holder.

Frustration buzzed through my body as I scraped my hand over my face.

There was a nine year age gap between Gabe and me. There'd never been any sibling rivalry, just a whole lot of hero worship on my part. If my big brother told me to do something, I was going to try like hell to do it.

I hopped out of my vehicle and grabbed my bat bag. I looked around but didn't see Meg yet.

Our city park was pretty decent. There was a basketball court, lots of running trails, a playground for the kids and best of all a few years ago they'd added a baseball field. Surprisingly, it didn't get a lot of use. It was probably too much trouble to scrounge up enough people for a game. Most people that wanted to practice went to the batting cages where their hits and pitches would be contained.

Knowing she'd find me at the field, I headed that way.

I'd expected her to resist my request to meet me. When she didn't I couldn't help but feel like we were making progress.

I'd contemplated the cages but the evening was too nice to be stuck inside.

As I dropped my bag on the ground I couldn't help but feel guilty about lying to my brother. He would never approve of what I was doing with Meg. Even if it was for a damn good reason.

"Where's the list?"

I'd been digging through my stuff and hadn't seen Meg walk up.

"The list?"

She nodded, causing the floppy bun on the back of her

head to wobble. "Apparently I need to add…'Meg must be at Luke's beck and call.'"

Ball and glove in hand, I stood to face her. "You didn't have to show up."

Her brows furrowed, as if she hadn't realized that.

Huh. Maybe I needed to loosen up a bit. I wasn't the control freak she seemed to think I was.

She jammed her hands onto her hips as she glanced around. "Who are we putting on a show for?"

I couldn't tell her I couldn't go home so I'd called her because I was bored.

I motioned to the busy street. "You never know when someone's going to drive by." Already I thought I'd seen Jaclyn once, but I'd caught just a glimpse. I was probably being paranoid. When I first broke up with her, she followed me around, always hassled me. "Now that you're here…" I held up the ball. "We might as well have some fun."

"Fun?"

I slapped a hand over my chest, the one holding my glove. "Your skepticism hurts."

She scratched her temple. "Okay then, let the forced fun begin."

"If you don't want to be here, I'm open to ideas. Did you have something else in mind?"

"I guess not."

"Let's go then." I tossed my ball and glove toward the pitcher's mound. Swiping up my bat, I led her to home plate.

"The key to a good, solid hit is to hold the bat correctly. You want to remember to hold it in your fingertips, not the palm of your hands."

I demonstrated the proper stance before handing the bat to her. She took it with an amused smile.

Progress.

Feeling encouraged, I moved behind her. My arms slid

around her body until my hands rested over her hands. Her body tensed as it pressed against mine. She was so close her hair tickled my cheek. The scent of her perfume about knocked me senseless. Or maybe it was the way her form curved into mine so perfectly that had me feeling lightheaded.

"Relax." I wasn't sure if the command was for her...or me. "Save all your power for the swing. You want to pull the bat back like this." Keeping my hands over hers, I guided the bat backward. My left arm crossed over her body, pressing her even more tightly against my chest. I heard her breath catch, so before I made her too uncomfortable, I guided her through a swing.

We ran through the motions a few more times before I stepped away.

"Make sure you keep your eye on the ball."

Meg looked at me like I was an idiot. "You're supposed to be this baseball superstar. That's the best advice you have? What, you think I'm going to start bird watching?"

"It might seem *obvious*," I retorted, "but you'd be surprised at how many people, especially girls, cringe and close their eyes when the ball is headed their way."

"Especially *girls*?"

I grinned. I loved getting her fired up. "Yeah."

"You know this?"

"I coach sometimes."

She gritted her teeth, her hands clenched the bat, and she dug her feet in, perfectly mimicking the stance I'd shown her.

I jogged to the mound where I swiped up my ball and glove. I slammed the ball into my palm a few times, pretending to warm up. Mostly, I was just admiring the view. She looked damn hot, her expression fierce as she waited for my pitch. I'd fired her up all right.

I wound up and then let go with far less force than I was used to.

Meg let loose, executing a perfect swing. The bat connected, the sound echoing beautifully through the park. My head snapped up as I watched the ball fly over, not landing until it was well into the outfield.

Sure, I threw her the perfect, easy pitch. But *damn…*

I'd caught the split-second smirk she quickly covered with her hand. She gave me a wide-eyed look, pretending to be surprised.

I stalked over to her. "What the hell was that?"

"Beginner's luck?" Her tone oozed mock innocence.

"Beginner's luck, my ass."

"I don't know what you mean." Her eyelashes fluttered, rendering me momentarily speechless. Who knew Meg Matthews had a playful side?

"Let's try that again." I returned to the mound, throwing a toss almost identical to the first. It arced, descending straight toward the sweet spot on the bat.

Meg swung, dropping the bat comically low as she ducked out of the way of the ball. I knew she was doing it on purpose, not wanting to gift me with another hit like the first. What she didn't count on was dropping the bat so low that she ended up stepping on it, tripping over it, and plopping backward onto her butt.

Her laughter caught me by surprise.

"You deserve that." I loped up to her, reaching out both hands. She grabbed hold, and I tugged her to her feet. "You lied to me."

I wasn't used to a girl being able to look me in the eye so easily. I still held her hands in mine. It didn't allow for much distance between us.

I'd dated my fair share of girls. All of them pretty, and they knew it. Every single one of them chose to flaunt it. Meg was different. She had an understated beauty. Sure, I'd noticed her before the night at the school. But I hadn't *really* noticed her.

Not the way I was noticing her now. Her eyes were as dark as coffee, her lips full, and her skin creamy and smooth. The contrast with her red hair made her look almost exotic.

She looked damn near flawless.

I realized I was staring when she tugged her hands away.

"Who said it was a lie?"

She twisted away from me, heading for the benches.

"Not so fast." I ordered. "You said you hate sports." Was I shocked that she lied? Nope. Getting information from her had been like squeezing a compliment out of my father. Damn near impossible.

I jogged after her, scrubbing my hand vigorously over her butt when I reached her.

"Hey." She swatted at me.

"Just helping out. You want to walk around with your backside covered in dirt?"

"Oh." She gave herself a few good swipes.

"What's the story here?"

We dropped down on a bench.

"I played softball in middle school. Soccer, too."

"Why'd you quit? You must've been pretty good."

She shrugged. "I was okay. Stuff came up. Life happens. I guess what I hate about sports is that I had to give them up."

Her expression clouded over. I wanted the smiling Meg to come back.

"Paint any more murals lately?"

Her gaze snapped to mine. The fire was back in her eyes. "No."

"I can't believe your parents let you ride a motorcycle. I can't think of a single girl I've dated who would've gotten away with that. Your parents must be really laid back to not care."

"They *care*," she said a bit defiantly, as if my words had been an insult.

Intuition told me I'd accidentally poked a sore spot. Curiosity made me poke it again. It seemed to be the best way to keep her talking. "Really?" I let doubt cloud my voice.

"My dad got his first motorcycle when he was sixteen. He's pretty much always had one. When I was a kid, he used to take me riding all the time. It was just…a normal part of life." She got a faraway look. It took her a few heartbeats to come back. "Mom was never a fan, but Dad always argued that they were safe." She shrugged. "When I decided to start riding, Dad wasn't thrilled, but what could he say?"

"I suppose it would be sexist of him to tell you not to when he did."

"Exactly. And he was younger than I was when he started riding." A smile tilted up one corner of her lips.

"What?"

"Would you still think the Rebel is sexy if you knew it belonged to him?"

"Uh…" I tried not to get a visual on that, not wanting the original to be ruined.

"It was just sitting in the garage, collecting dust. I needed a way to get around. I missed riding. I was comfortable on it, and familiar with it. I thought, why not?" She frowned. "He put up a bit of a fight, but my arguments wore him down."

"And now look at you, cruising around on your crime-mobile."

"Would you stop?" She shoved me so hard I almost fell off the bench. The spark in her eyes kept me going.

"How is it that your parents let you go out at night?"

"Who says they let me?"

"You little rebel you." I gave her a much softer shove than she'd given me. "They don't hear you coming and going?"

She scrunched up her face. I was becoming familiar with that look. She was debating whether or not she was going to tell me something.

"I walk the Rebel down the block before I start it. Then walk it home." She scowled at me but it was missing its usual bite. "Just so you know, it's not like I go out all that much. I don't paint nearly as often as you seem to think. But once in a while I just like to get away."

"Yeah. I can relate to that."

Her stomach growled.

Loudly.

"Maebelle's?" I asked, half expecting her to decline.

"Sure. I'm dying for some onion rings."

We gathered up my gear and loaded it into my vehicle.

I pulled the notebook out and dug for something to write with. I found a broken pencil.

She groaned. "What are you doing?"

"Making a rule for you." I started to scribble.

Meg will feel incredible remorse for lying to Luke about her athletic ability.

"It's blasphemous," I added.

"Blasphemous?" She snorted.

"Baseball is sacred."

Chapter Eight

Meg

The industrial paint mixer emitted a laborious sound as it meticulously shook the can of paint. The frazzled lady who had dashed in minutes ago, trying to beat closing time, flipped through a book of wallpaper samples as she waited.

I reached under the counter for an extra paint stick.

When I popped my head up, Luke was standing at the back of the store. The machine had drowned out the dinging of the bell. Noting I was busy with a customer, he began to wander. He plucked a can of spray paint off the display and held it in the air, shook it, and then mimed painting a mural on the window. I reflexively clenched my jaw, assuming he was mocking me. When he didn't look at me once, I realized maybe he was just…trying it out? He seemed to be enjoying himself.

Our charade had been going on for a few weeks now. He had never stopped by before. This was another topic that hadn't been touched on yet. My fingers itched, wanting to scribble in that green notebook.

When the machine stopped rumbling, I twisted around, pulling the can from its now silent clutches.

"Here you are." I held out the can of Plum Dandy along with the extra paint sticks. "It's ready to go, but you can take these in case you need to do any touching up later."

"Thank you." She scurried toward the entrance. Luke stepped in front of her, opening the door. "What a gentleman."

I rolled my eyes. *Show off.*

"What are you doing here?" I demanded as he strode up to the counter.

"Can't I stop by for a second?"

"I'm working."

He glanced around the empty store. Not in a snide way, but more as if he was confused as to how that could be a problem. "You don't look too busy at the moment. Can we talk?" He didn't wait for an answer. "There's something I want to give you."

He handed me a white envelope.

"What's this?"

"A gift. For you. Open it."

I hesitated, not wanting anything from him.

"Just open it."

I did as commanded. Two tickets slid out. The heavy ivory paper was embossed in gold writing. I quickly scanned the invitation before giving him a questioning look.

"They're tickets for some art gala in the city," he clarified.

Sapphire Bay was a half hour drive to the south. It was the biggest city in the area.

"I gathered as much." I grimaced. "We have to go to this? Are you planning on boring me into compliance?"

His smile disappeared. "No. I thought you'd want to go."

"Oh, right." Too late I remembered he'd told me it was a gift.

"You don't look happy."

I shook my head in confusion. I had no idea what to say. I could tell I'd hurt his feelings.

"I thought it would be something you would enjoy," he said. "You're into art, aren't you?"

"I'm not," I admitted.

"You don't like art?"

"Not really. But we can totally go," I offered.

"*I* don't want to go," he said. "I thought *you* would. If you don't like art then what's with the…" He faded off as he mimed spraying with a can of paint again.

I swatted his hand back down to his side. "Stop doing that. And no, art has nothing to do with it."

"Then what—"

"It's not something I want to talk about."

"Fine." He took the fancy tickets and stuffed them back into the envelope. "I'll give them to my parents or something."

I felt an unwanted twinge of guilt. "I'm sorry, Luke. The thought was really sweet."

"Sweet?" His smile flickered back into place.

Dang. He had a nice smile.

I looked away, checking out the clock behind me.

"You should probably go so I can lock up."

Ignoring me, he moved through the store, following as I flipped off the lights.

"Actually, could you come over?"

My mind whirred into action. "Sure."

He narrowed his eyes at me. "That was too easy."

"I don't have to."

"No. I want you to. Adam and Trevor are going to stop by later. It will look good if we're hanging out."

My parents weren't speaking at the moment. The house echoed with their deafening silence. I could hardly stand it. But it annoyed me that I'd rather spend time with the boy who was blackmailing me. Still, every time he asked, I found myself willing to go.

There was another perk of going to Luke's. Maybe if I spent some time in his domain, I could dig up some dirt on him. What better place to look for aforementioned dirt than in his bedroom? What if I could find something I could use against him? What if I could blackmail him right back?

"Can I meet you there?"

"Sure."

Closing up the store didn't take long. The ride to Luke's didn't take long, either. As I cruised into the circular drive, I belatedly contemplated what his parents would think about a girl on a motorcycle zooming up to their house. I realized I didn't particularly care. What could they do? Forbid him from seeing me? I could only hope.

I wasn't sure where to park. I came to a stop next to the walkway that led to the front door. Most likely it wasn't the most appropriate place, which made it perfect for me.

I told myself there was no reason to be nervous. I had no one to impress.

So what if Luke's house was an enormous brick monstrosity? So what if his last girlfriend's purse collection was worth more than my entire wardrobe?

Before I could ring the bell, the door was tugged open.

"You made it."

"You doubted me?" He practically owned me. Of course I was going to do what he asked.

For now.

He flicked his head to the side, signaling that I should enter.

I felt like I was walking into another world—or at least a world completely different from my own. The heels of my boots clicked on the marble floor of the massive foyer. A staircase rose to the upper level and curved back down again.

A chandelier glinted overhead. Uncomfortable ogling what this guy thought was normal, I swiveled my attention back to him.

"Let's head to my room." He led the way up the massive staircase. I followed him to the end of the hallway, where he shoved open a door. He motioned for me to go through first.

This was his bedroom? Apartments were smaller than this. A king-size bed with a matching bedroom set took up one side of the enormous space. A black leather couch acted as a divider between the sleeping area and the living area. There was also a recliner at an angle. All the better to get a view of the enormous flat screen that hung on the wall. A black lacquered coffee table was in front of the sofa. It was covered with homework.

"Should I grab drinks? Or are you hungry?"

"Actually," I made an apologetic face, seizing the opportunity, "I'm starving. I always eat when I get off work."

It wasn't even a lie.

"No problem. I'll be right back. Maybe you can find something for us to watch. The remote is next to the TV. Check out the movie channels if you want."

He didn't close the door. I scampered over and peeked into the hallway. I could hear his footsteps padding down the staircase.

I darted back into his room. His dresser seemed like an obvious place to start. A foray into his underwear drawer produced not a lot more than, well, underwear—boxer briefs, to be exact. He also had an absurd amount of socks. And aside from a couple of jock straps, there wasn't much else to see.

I wiped my hands on my leggings, ridding myself of unseen germs.

I hurriedly rifled through the lower drawers but they were even more boring.

His nightstand was next. It produced a flashlight, a stack

of *Sports Illustrated*, random writing utensils, and a few college brochures. The brochures sat at a suspicious angle. I pushed them aside, exposing an open box of condoms.

I froze as my heart did an unexpected dip, skydiving into my stomach. My traitorous mind taunted me with a flashback of the night on the baseball field. When Luke had his arms around me, when I'd been caged against his body, it had felt blissful. An unwanted ache coursed through me as I thought about being tangled up in Luke's arms again.

I slammed the drawer shut.

How messed up was I? The boy was blackmailing me.

I blamed it on hormones. Stupid, traitorous hormones.

I let out a growl of frustration as I darted over to the closed door that was off his bedroom. It opened into a closet.

There were enough clothes in here to fill a small boutique.

"Unbelievable," I whispered. Everything was arranged meticulously. Long-sleeve button downs arranged by color, then short-sleeve button downs arranged by color. Next came sweaters, again, arranged by color followed by shirts of a more casual nature. At the end of the line were at least a dozen suits and…yes, two tuxedos.

I wasn't sure if I was impressed or appalled.

The boy owned more shoes than any one boy should be allowed to own.

A small table stood just inside the door. Two crooked piles of books were stacked on top of it. I assumed the eclectic pile was tucked away so as not to mar the perfection of his bedroom. He had *Moby Dick*, several titles by Stephen King, and what looked like a wide variety of everything in between.

A copy of *Little Women* had a blue highlighter sticking out of it.

Perplexing, but not exactly blackmail worthy.

I backed out of the closet, disappointed by its lack of secret hiding places.

"Whatcha doin'?"

I shrieked.

"You scared me," I scolded as I twisted around. "I was looking for the bathroom."

He held a serving tray in his hands. He motioned with his head toward the door that led off from the sitting area. "It's that way."

"Right. Okay." I backed the rest of the way out of his closet and pulled the door shut.

I couldn't bear to look at him as I crossed the room and disappeared behind the bathroom door. Once inside, I rested against it. I pressed my hand against my thundering heart, willing it to slow down.

I wasn't sure what I had been hoping to find. I was pretty sure he wasn't a pothead. Everyone had made it clear he was some kind of star ball player. Steroids maybe? If I found them, would I even know what I was looking at? Or maybe he'd cheated on Jaclyn. Or tests. Maybe he'd cheated on tests. It didn't seem fair that a guy that looked like him, was as athletic as he was, and lived in a house like this should also have brains to boot.

Maybe he had a stash of purchased homework somewhere.

I knew I wouldn't find anything in his bathroom. They undoubtedly had a housekeeper. He wouldn't be stupid enough to keep anything incriminating in his room.

So maybe on his laptop?

Or his phone.

I flushed the toilet for show, and then scrubbed my hands on principal.

By the time I emerged from the bathroom Luke had settled on the couch. He balanced a plate in one hand while peeking at his phone with the other.

He hadn't left the phone in his room when he went to the kitchen. How was I ever supposed to get it away from him? Besides, it was probably password protected. Come to think of it, his laptop was likely protected as well. My earlier determination began to fizzle into a state of dejection.

He patted the spot on the couch next to him. "Dinner's served."

It sure was.

I was momentarily speechless. I'd expected something along the lines of chips and salsa. Instead he'd taken the time to make sandwiches. Crusty croissants layered with ham, cheese, lettuce, and tomatoes. Spears of pickles rested on the plate.

"I figured if you like root beer, you like root beer floats."

"Love them almost as much as hot chocolate."

He nudged me and widened his eyes in mock-surprise. "We have another thing in common. *I* love them almost as much as cookie sundaes."

I shook my head. "Thanks for dinner. You really didn't have to go to so much trouble."

"You said you were hungry, and I can always eat." He shrugged. "I wasn't sure what you like on your sandwich. I brought up mayo and honey mustard. If you want something else, I could probably find it for you."

I settled in next to him. "No. This is good. I'm not picky."

"Look at you, being all agreeable," Luke teased. His knee playfully bounced against mine. "I think you might be starting to like me, at least a little."

I thought maybe he was right.

Chapter Nine

LUKE

"What can I get you?" The woman behind the counter let her gaze bounce between Meg and me. Common Grounds was only a few blocks from school. It was a coffee shop with a full bakery. It got a lot of business this time of day.

It was the perfect place for us to make an appearance.

"Two cookie sundaes," I said. The woman tapped the order onto the screen. "And two large milks." Can't have cookies without milk.

I paid and we waited at the end of the counter for our food. Moments later two plates were handed to us. Each held an enormous chocolate chip cookie buried under two scoops of ice cream. Hot fudge oozed down the sides, creating a molten pool around the entire dessert.

Meg moaned theatrically. "That looks *so* good. I bet it's worth all the calories."

"It is," I assured her. I grabbed both plates, and she grabbed our milk. "It's my favorite dessert in the world."

"Is this booth okay?" she asked.

"Sure." It was near the front door, the best place to make ourselves noticed.

I set our plates down but didn't drop into my seat. Meg's shoulder bumped mine as she put our milks on the table. Not a single day had gone by that I didn't notice the perfume she wore. When she got out of my SUV, her scent lingered. Standing this close to her, it was all I could do not to lean in to get a good whiff.

Meg's animosity was starting to fade. I didn't think sniffing her was a good way to win her over, but damn, the girl smelled good.

"What kind of perfume do you wear?" The words shot out of my mouth. I slid into the booth and grabbed my fork, trying to pretend I wasn't dying to hear her answer.

She already had a fork in hand, a gooey bite lifted halfway to her mouth. She lowered it as she narrowed her eyes at me. Apparently she didn't appreciate the question.

"Why?" She immediately sounded defensive. "Is it too strong? Does it smell cheap? What's wrong with it?"

I held up my hands in surrender. "There's nothing wrong with it. Whatever it is, it's the perfect scent for you. It's sweet but not too sweet. It has an edge of zing to it."

"Zing?"

"Kinda sweet, yet spunky."

"It's apricot vanilla."

"Yeah it is." Now that she said it, I totally knew what it was. "I like it."

"Thank you?"

"You're welcome. I like having a girlfriend who smells good."

"You smell pretty good yourself."

Her eyes quickly flicked away from mine. Her cheeks reddened. I was pretty sure she wished she could take back her words. I knew I could razz her about this, or I could maybe gain some points by letting it go.

It was enough that she liked my cologne.

Okay, so maybe blackmail wasn't a great way to win someone over. But I had no choice. I wondered if I'd met her under different circumstances if she would still think of me as a spoiled jock.

Luke Prescott, spoiled rich kid. Meg's words echoed through my mind far too often.

I didn't want her to think of me as a spoiled anything. Least of all a spoiled *Prescott.* If I had my way, I'd have nothing to do with my family name. Part of me wanted to tell her that. The logical side of my brain won out. Jumping into that explanation would tear the cover off a whole crate of issues I didn't want to discuss.

The bell over the door jingled. Meg corkscrewed her neck trying to see who entered. I knew she was hoping it was Francesca. She had asked if her friend could join us, and I didn't have a good reason to tell her no. Again, maybe I was trying to gain some points with this chick.

It wasn't Francesca who strolled in. It was several of my teammates. They all called out a greeting. A few greeted Meg as well. She gave them a tentative smile.

"I need to talk to you about something." I leaned across the table. I wanted to toss this out there before her friend showed.

"Okay?"

"Next Friday night you're meeting my parents."

I was met with a wide-eyed look. "No, I'm not."

"Yes, you are. There's an event I need to attend. It's a charity ball. Down in Sapphire Bay. Mom is being given an award because of the fundraising she's done. I'm required to go, and I'm expected to bring a date. Since you *are* my girlfriend…" I let the unfinished sentence hang in the air.

This was non-negotiable—unlike the art gala—which I was actually relieved she turned down because *boring*. Not that I anticipated the ball being anything less than torturous, but I needed her there.

"A charity ball?" She shook her head so hard a few strands of her ponytail came free. "There's no way. That's just...not my kind of thing. Count me out. I agreed to spend some evenings with you. I agreed to show off our relationship at school. I never agreed to *events* involving parents."

My parents' presence was exactly *why* I needed her to go. I couldn't let her talk her way out of this. I had too much riding on it. I leaned across the table, keeping my voice low. "Are you forgetting the deal we made? If I say you're going, you're going."

She seemed to wilt under the forcefulness of my words. I hated playing hardball, but she wasn't giving me a choice.

"And if I refuse?" Her tone was icy.

"Pretty sure you know the answer to that."

"You'd turn me in," she said flatly.

I gave her a pointed look.

"I can't believe I was actually starting to think you were a nice guy." She shoved her dessert away.

"Meg." She refused to look at me. "I don't know why you're so pissy. We had a deal."

"Yes." She crossed her arms over her chest and glared at me. "Thank you *so* much for the reminder."

I glanced around. My teammates were a few tables away.

"People are going to think we're fighting."

"Maybe because we are." She didn't relent. "I know we had a deal. But that doesn't mean you get to use that arrogant, entitled tone with me. Whatever happened to asking nicely?"

"If I'd asked nicely, would you have agreed?"

Her clenched jaw was my answer.

"Yeah. Didn't think so."

I burned with frustration. Meg had finally started to warm up to me, but now her animosity was back full-force. So much for gaining points with her today. I'd just shoved us back to square one. And I had no one to blame but myself. In that moment, I reminded myself of my dad. I'd just bullied her in order to get my way, proving I was the spoiled kid she accused me of being.

I didn't want to be that person.

My whole life I'd fought *against* being that person.

"Look," I said in the most reasonable tone I could scrounge up, "I'm sorry. You're right. I should've asked nicely. It's just that I need you to go, and I was sure you'd say no."

She eyed me suspiciously. "Are they expecting you to bring Jaclyn?"

"Mom didn't say that, exactly," I hedged.

"But she assumes?"

I shrugged. "How should I know what that woman is thinking?"

"That woman? You mean your mom?"

"We're not exactly close," I admitted. "She told me to bring a date. That was pretty much the end of the discussion."

"It's a ball? Like with actual ball gowns?"

Ball gowns? "I don't know. I guess. I mean, yeah, the ladies all wear dresses."

She reached over, picked up her spoon, and began swirling it through the melted ice cream.

"So, are we good?"

She lifted her gaze to mine. Her expression was blank.

"If by 'good' you mean to ask if I'm going to do what you say, then sure. What choice do I have?"

"Meg, I really don't want it to be this way." How could my dad stand to have so many people hate him? Having this one girl pissed at me was enough to drive me crazy.

"Meg!" Francesca exclaimed as she slid into the booth.

Her hip bumped Meg's, nudging her over. "I'm sorry I'm so late. I was FaceTime-ing with Nate and lost track of time." She turned to me. "Hey, Luke. Oh my gosh." She eyed up my sundae. "That looks divine."

"I'll go get you one." I slid out of the booth before she had a chance to protest. I needed a breather. It was no secret that Jaclyn was high maintenance—and proud of it. When I first put my plan into motion I never would've guessed that Meg would be even more so, in a completely different way.

Jaclyn clung to me like a barnacle on a ship.

Meg was like one of those wild horses insistent on fighting me every step of the way.

Her assessment of me ate away at me. I was determined to win her over, make her see I wasn't the jackass she thought.

I leaned against the counter, waiting on the dessert.

Meg was speaking animatedly with Francesca, her hands flying in the air.

The words "ball" and "hoity-toity" floated over to me. The rest of the conversation was lost.

The waitress handed me a plate. The girls' jabbering faded as I neared the table.

"Thank you," Francesca said.

"No problem." I sat down to tackle the melted mess that had been my dessert.

Meg continued to pick at hers.

I tried to strike up a conversation with Francesca. "How's Nate these days?"

She looked at me in confusion as she hurriedly swallowed the bite she'd stuffed into her mouth. "Good. You know Nate?"

"Yeah, we worked on some stuff together last summer."

"Stuff?" Meg echoed.

I evaded her question. "Nate's a great guy."

Francesca smiled. "He really is."

"Hey, Prescott."

The three of us turned to a table clear across the room. My teammates were crowded around it. Their table was littered with empty plates and half-filled glasses.

"What's up, Darren?" I called back.

"We were thinking about heading over to the batting cages. You in?"

"Nah, I'm busy."

Meg reached across the table and placed her hand over mine. "You should go."

"Yeah, you should." Colton chortled. "Listen to your girl, Luke."

The guys got up from their table in a cacophony of screeching chairs, pressing me to join them.

"You don't mind?" Mind? She was still fuming. I knew she was anxious to be rid of me but we had an audience that didn't know better.

She gave me a sweet smile that almost looked real. "Not at all."

I smirked. "Of course you don't." I turned to my group of friends who were now standing next to our table. "I'm in."

"Awesome," Colton said.

"That girl's a keeper." Darren ruffled Meg's hair. "I like her."

"So do I." I leaned across the table, framing her cheeks in my hands as I gave her a loud, obnoxious kiss.

The guys groaned.

Francesca scowled.

Meg blushed.

Mission accomplished.

"If we're gonna do this, let's jet."

• • •

"Lucas." Dad bellowed, stopping me in my tracks.

The batting cages had been the perfect stress reliever. I hadn't been home two minutes and I felt as if every muscle in my body was taut enough to snap. I owed that to the man stomping down the hallway.

"Yeah?" I twisted around on the staircase and descended the few steps I'd climbed.

"Anything you want to tell me?"

"Not really." My belligerence was met with a red-faced scowl.

"You got a B on your Trig test."

"It was a B-plus," I corrected. I really hated that our school had grades available online. It seemed Dad checked them hourly.

"It's unacceptable, that's what it is," he shot back. "You want to play ball this spring? You best not let that happen again. You need a parent's signature to play. I won't sign if I think your grades will be affected."

My spine stiffened. Dad used baseball as leverage every chance he got. And why wouldn't he? It was the one thing he knew would always work.

"If I don't get another B this term, can I go to the camp in Colorado?"

He huffed in contempt. "Not a chance. You know how I feel about wasting my money on that nonsense."

"I don't need your money! I just need your signature," I argued. "What's so bad about sending me to a training camp?"

"I've told you. It's a waste of time. You need to start concentrating on your future." He turned and walked away from me, the conversation apparently over.

I glared at his back. I *was* concentrating on my future. A future different than the one he had planned for me.

Chapter Ten

MEG

I had spent days fretting over the charity ball. Francesca and I had looked up last year's ball online. Where was I ever going to find an appropriate dress? Francesca suggested the clearance racks. I knew what clearance racks were like. They were flooded with extra-extra smalls and extra-extra larges. The sizes most people didn't quite wear. I already knew I was going to stand out like, well, like a leather-clad biker chick at a black tie art gala. I shoved the worry aside. There would be plenty of time to stress over it later.

Right now I wished it was my biggest concern as I stared at the poster on the wall. The school was plastered with them. Brightly colored pages boasting a reward for any information that led to…me.

I shuddered.

"Meg?"

I twisted around, feeling insanely guilty.

Miss Perez's eyes widened. "Are you okay?"

"Yes." I clapped a hand over my heart. "You just startled me."

"Sorry about that. Come on in."

Her office was oddly comforting. The walls were boring beige, the flooring industrial style linoleum. Her desk was as cluttered as ever. The bookshelf behind her dripped books and pages from binders.

I dropped into the brown leather chair. It was lumpy, squeaky, and had definitely seen better days. I'd logged a lot of hours in this chair.

"How are you?"

"I'm good."

I smiled, hoping it was not a guilty looking smile.

She perched her glasses on top of her head. "I'm glad to hear that. Now that the year is underway I wanted to touch base with you. How are classes going?"

"Good," I said sincerely. "I feel more focused this year."

"Wonderful. Have you given any more thought to what colleges you would like to apply to?"

"I think I'm going to stick to the state colleges we discussed last spring."

"Perfect. I've assembled some information on scholarships and financial aid." She slid a folder toward me. Most likely I would qualify for need-based financial assistance, but there was no guarantee. If not, even a state college bypassed the limits of what my family could afford. I cringed at the thought of asking my parents for money. We hadn't discussed college *ever*. It was clear money was tight, and I didn't want to add to that burden. I saw student loans in my near future—but if that was what it took, so be it.

"Thank you." I took the folder and placed it on my lap.

She leaned forward, elbows on the desk, and stacked her fingers beneath her chin. "Meg, is there something bothering you?"

"What?" I thought I'd hidden it so well.

She smiled vaguely at my surprise. "Is there something you would like to talk about?"

I hesitated.

"How are Rick and Marion?" she pressed.

A confession spilled forth.

She listened raptly as I told her about my parents. Their arguing had fizzled into an unending silence. History told me it would loop back around to fighting again.

"Marion is still struggling," she guessed.

"My dad is reaching the end of his patience." I felt guilty for the admission. "I mean, he's still patient. He's just… frustrated."

"And you? How does this situation make you feel?"

Scared. Anxious. Sad. "Frustrated," I decided. "Frustrated in a lot of ways."

"How so?"

Where did I begin?

"I want them to work things out." That was a blanket statement that summed up everything in a nice, neat little package.

Time flew by as I voiced all my concerns.

"Would you mind if I gave Marion a call? Perhaps I can suggest a support group?"

"Dad's already tried."

"Sometimes it helps if suggestions come from an outsider. There's less pressure. Fewer expectations to meet."

"Then by all means, give it a go." I doubted Mom would be receptive to her. Then again, I hadn't thought I would be receptive to her, either, back when I first started seeing her. But Miss Perez had a calming way about her.

The last bell of the day shrilled in the hallway.

"Is there anything else?" I asked.

"I don't know, is there?"

I smiled at her subtle, yet familiar, way of pressing me. "No. Not today."

"If you need anything, you know where to find me."

Miss Perez's office was on the opposite side of the school from my locker. By the time I reached it, Luke was leaned against it scanning the crowd with a sulky look on his face. He perked up when he saw me.

"Where were you?" he asked. "I waited outside of English."

"Sorry." I turned away from him as I tackled my locker comb. "I wasn't there."

"Obviously. Julia said she thought she heard you were excused to go to the guidance counselor."

"I was." I stuffed my books inside my locker and wiggled into my leather jacket.

"Why? Is something wrong? Does she know about...?"

I could imagine where that sentence had been headed. *Does she know about the graffiti?* Or, *Does she know about the blackmail?*

"She wanted to talk to me about a few options for college."

His brow furrowed. "College?"

I hiked my messenger bag up my shoulder and turned to him.

"If you must know, I requested a meeting with her to discuss options for student loans, scholarships, and financial aid. *Some of us*," I grated out, "have to worry about those things."

His head snapped back, as if my words had smacked him upside the head. "You think you're the only one who worries about those things?"

"Paying for college? No. A lot of us do. Just not *you*." I took off walking, suddenly irritated with him because of the simple fact that his family had money and college would not be an issue for him.

"You were in there a long time."

"I wanted her advice. I think I want to be a guidance counselor." I *knew* I wanted to be a guidance counselor. We'd talked about it at length last spring. Luke didn't need to know that today's discussion revolved around my family.

"Really?"

I forgave him for sounding so shocked. He had no way of knowing how much Miss Perez had helped me over the years. No way of knowing that I would like to pay it forward someday.

"Really," I said. "Is it so crazy to want to help people?"

"I think it's great."

He sounded like he meant it.

He pushed open the door, and we walked out into the sunshine.

In plain view, leaning up against a silver sports car, was Jaclyn. Trevor, one of the guys we'd had pizza with, was wedged against her. They were in the midst of a full on lip lock. Never mind that it was against school rules, it was also tacky and just plain...*ick*.

I nudged Luke. "Does that bother you?"

"What, them? Not in the way you think." He shuddered. "Every time I see her in a situation like that it makes me realize I really dodged a bullet."

"You know chances are that display is for your benefit." We looped around them, keeping our distance.

"I know." He grimaced. "I feel kind of bad that she's willing to make such a fool of herself on my account."

I reflexively looked over my shoulder, immediately wishing I hadn't.

Without Luke as an audience, Jaclyn's show was officially over. She scowled at me as our eyes met. I quickly turned around and let Luke lead me to his vehicle.

I hopped into the front seat. We were meeting Adam and

Julia at Common Grounds.

He slid inside but didn't start it up right away. "I bought you something."

I turned to look at him, suspicion flowing through me. "Really?"

"Yes."

"What is it this time? Opera tickets? A night at the ballet?" I teased. Since our argument about the charity ball he'd been going out of his way to be even nicer than usual.

"Funny girl. No. This time I got you something you need. You might not like it," he warned, "but you need it."

He leaned across me, opened the glove compartment, and pulled out a hot pink vial. It had a spray nozzle on top.

"Perfume? I thought you liked the scent I wear." Was he just trying to be polite before? Did it smell cheap, after all?

"I do. *This* isn't perfume. It's pepper spray," he corrected.

"For…?"

"You. For when you're out late at night."

"I don't need pepper spray."

"I think you do." He reached over and unzipped my jacket pocket. Before I could ask him what he was doing he'd stuffed the spray inside and zipped me back up. He gave my pocket a pat as if to prove his point.

He poked a finger at me. "Keep it in there. You never know when you might need it."

• • •

"I got your text," I told Francesca. "Your mom let me in."

She wore a huge smile as she tugged me into her room. "I found a dress for you."

"Seriously?" My voice squeaked with excitement.

"It's my nonna's."

"Your grandma's?" I attempted to keep my voice even.

My mind was suddenly flooded with lots of gaudy sequins, an abundance of lace, and frumpily fitting styles. "Oh."

"Trust me. You know Nonna is a borderline hoarder." She shook her head. "Doesn't matter. What matters is that I think you'll love it."

I had met Francesca's nonna. She was a pleasantly plump woman with ebony hair, courtesy of Clairol. She always smelled vaguely of garlic. She adored blue eye shadow and giving hugs.

Was there a polite way to tell your friend that wearing her grandmother's dress held about as much appeal as wearing a curtain? If there was, I couldn't think of it.

Francesca darted into her walk-in closet. With a flourish she came out, holding up a vintage dress for my inspection.

Black organza covered a bright aqua, satin slip dress. The color reminded me of Luke's eyes. The underlying color was visible enough to give it a nudge from pretty into gorgeous. Black glitter piping shimmered in a swirling pattern. The dress was cinched at the waist. The calf length skirt flared out in a classic cupcake style.

It was beautiful.

"You should try it on. Nonna was busty, even back then," Francesca said. "She told me if she needs to take it in a bit for you, she would do that."

"Your nonna's a seamstress?" I took the dress from her.

She shook her head. "Not really. She believes domestic skills are a lost art. The woman loves to bake, sew, and I swear, even clean."

She turned around to give me a modicum of privacy. I shimmied out of my jeans and tugged off my shirt, letting them fall to the floor. I carefully slid the dress over my head.

"Need help with the zipper?"

"Actually, I do." I held the plunging sweetheart neckline in place as Francesca zipped me up. She was right. It was a bit baggy in the chest. It wasn't treacherously loose, but loose enough to need some corrective action.

She tugged at the fabric. "She can fix that right up. I promise." She took a step back to get a better vantage point. Her eyes lit up. "You pull off vintage well. Maybe you should consider a new look."

Francesca placed her hands on my shoulders and guided me to the mirror over her dresser. I wasn't able to see all of myself, but what I did see, I liked.

"This is amazing." The dress was so unique I knew I wouldn't feel the urge to compare myself to anyone else.

"You *look* amazing," Francesca gushed. "I've already got some ideas about your hair and makeup. Come over that night and I'll help you get ready."

"That would be great." I wouldn't have to explain to my parents why I was getting all dressed up.

"We can go shopping for shoes. I saw the cutest pair of platform Mary Jane's. They would be *so* cute with this. I was also thinking you could wear that pair of oversize, black onyx studs your parents got you for your birthday."

"I like that idea." Again, it would be a look all my own. I wouldn't be competing against diamonds and pearls. The look Francesca was helping me put together was all *me*. I twisted away from the mirror and squeezed her into a hug. "You are the best friend ever."

"Hey, so, as long as we're on the topic of Luke—"

"We actually weren't on the topic of Luke," I corrected. "We were on the topic of nonnas and dresses and friendships."

"And we were swinging back around to Luke," she assured me.

"If you say so."

"Remember when he mentioned Nate and I asked how they knew each other?" she asked. "His answer was kind of evasive, so I asked Nate."

Had his answer been evasive? I couldn't remember. I had already been fretting about the ball.

"Okay," I said agreeably. "So then what?"

"He said they got to know each other this past summer because they were both working for an organization through Community Ed."

"What kind of organization?" I couldn't picture Luke being involved in the community in any way. I did recall Nate doing something this past summer. "Wait, was Luke part of the sports camp Nate worked at?" If I recalled correctly the organization worked with underprivileged youth.

"He was. Nate said he was good with the kids. The lead supervisor commented that he was disappointed by the lack of sports equipment. A few days later an anonymous shipment showed up. Nate said it had everything—footballs, soccer balls, and everything the kids would need for baseball."

"Baseball," I parroted.

"Baseball, as in Luke's passion," Francesca added.

"Luke donated all of that?"

"Nate wasn't positive it was Luke," she admitted. "Probably it was Luke's dad. Still. That has to mean Luke was at least behind it. Right?"

"Maybe. I wouldn't know." As soon as I said the words a memory flashed through my mind. I clearly pictured the bundle of baseball bats resting on the floor in his backseat. Was he *donating* those?

A blackmailing philanthropist? It seemed like an unlikely combination. Then I thought of the pepper spray in my pocket—not necessarily the cost of it, but the thoughtfulness behind it—and realized maybe it wasn't such a stretch.

Chapter Eleven

LUKE

My palms were sweating, and it wasn't entirely because of the ridiculous tux I had to wear. My mother had one of her infamous tantrums before I left the house. All week she'd been telling me I needed to ditch Meg so I could bring Jaclyn to the ball. No way was that happening.

I told Mom I was going with Meg, or I wasn't going at all. Obviously I had hoped for the "not going at all" option. Unfortunately Dad stepped in. He insisted this evening would be the perfect opportunity to meet my new "friend."

As much as I hated it, my parents meeting Meg was a pivotal part of my plan. No matter when it happened I knew it was too much to expect that they would treat her with decency. At best, they would treat her with disinterest. At worst, well, I couldn't go there.

I wanted Meg to make an impression on my parents. It didn't matter to me if it was a good one. Julia had hinted that Meg was worried about finding an appropriate dress. She was so belligerent I wouldn't have been surprised if she dressed for the ball in a leather mini and thigh high boots. Just to prove a point. Actually, I wouldn't mind seeing her in a mini and thigh-highs.

Luckily I didn't need my parents to approve of Meg, or even like her. After Mom's last tantrum I was feeling vindictive. I was so sick of hearing about Jaclyn. "Perfect" Jaclyn. I bounded up the steps to Francesca's house. This night could not get over fast enough. If I felt that way I could only imagine how much worse it was for my date.

I stabbed the doorbell and heard it reverberate through the house.

Francesca swung the door open, giving me a smug smile. "It's about time you got here."

"I'm right on time," I said.

With a flourish Francesca directed me to Meg.

Her hair was in a complicated, retro looking up do. She had worked some magic with her eye makeup. Her eyes were defined, and her lashes were miles long. Her dress looked like something out of an old black and white movie. End result? She looked like a cross between a Hollywood goddess and a 1950s pin-up girl.

I was afraid to open my mouth because I was pretty sure I'd need to scrape my jaw off the floor.

"What kind of date *are* you?" Francesca backhanded me across the chest. "Don't you have any manners? Tell your date how pretty she looks."

Pretty? Calling Meg "pretty" was like calling the universe "big." It just fell short.

Her dress was black, no surprise there. But peeking through from beneath was a vibrant shade of light blue. I swear, it set off the flame-like quality of her hair.

Meg shifted nervously from foot to foot as I tried to find my voice. Her teeth clamped down on her lower lip.

"You look…" I floundered for the right word. I'd always thought she was gorgeous. How did you improve on gorgeous? I didn't know. "You look so stunning. I'm kind of speechless."

"Are you sure?" she asked. "You're not just saying that? Just tell me if this look is all wrong. The dress is vintage so I thought it would be okay. I couldn't afford anything even close to the dresses people wore to last year's ball. I'm sorry. I didn't mean to ruin this for you. If you want, you can tell your parents I have the flu. We don't have to go," she rambled.

"You can't be serious," Francesca scolded in her version of a pep talk. "You look amazing. If you don't look good enough for meeting Luke's parents, then obviously they are not worth your time."

I wondered if she had any idea how true her words really were.

"You honestly look amazing," I said. "Everyone else will think so, too."

Meg's body was stiff as a statue as we made our way down Francesca's sidewalk. Poor girl didn't look like she was going to a ball. She looked like she was being led to the gallows.

• • •

The ball didn't start with dancing. It began with an elaborate meal. My parents were entangled in conversation with the other couple at the table. After a quick introduction, they had treated Meg and me like we were invisible. It was for the best. I had nothing to contribute to the conversation. Meg looked overwhelmed trying to decide which piece of silverware to use for each course, and I caught her giving me sidelong glances. I tried to make it easy for her to follow my lead.

I also caught her glancing around the ballroom of the historic hotel with a completely awed look on her face. She was taking in the obscenely low-cut dresses, the pompous decorations, the elaborately set tables. All things I'd never really paid attention to before.

Eventually the Sinclairs excused themselves so they could say hello to another couple. As soon as they were gone I muttered, "Good riddance."

"Lucas," Mom snapped. "That was rude."

"Aw, come on," I grumbled. "I can't be the only one tired of listening to Lyle ramble on about the injustice of having to offer his employees healthcare. The guy's a pretentious ass hat."

"*Lucas*." My mother's voice was a low, sharp warning.

"What?" I shrugged. "Dad thinks so."

Dad smirked. "And yet I have enough sense to not announce it in a public place."

"No one is paying attention," I argued. "I don't think I have anything to worry about."

"Do you want our attention?" Mom's tone was condescending.

"Not particularly," I admitted. "But maybe you could take a little time to get to know my date."

Meg had barely said a word but she turned to me now, looking horrified.

My father eyed her with curiosity while my mother did nothing to hide her distaste. She forced a pinched-looking smile. "Meg, why don't you tell us about yourself?"

Meg fidgeted with her napkin. She opened her mouth but quickly snapped it shut.

"Meg." I gave her thigh a gentle nudge.

"I like spending time at the ocean," she blurted out. "And watching old movies."

"Ah," Mom said. "I suppose that explains the dress."

It wasn't exactly an insult. But it sure wasn't a compliment.

"I think the girl looks pretty damn good," Dad chuckled.

I flinched but knew better than to reprimand my father. It

would only make matters worse. If possible it was always best to ignore him so the matter would drop.

"What else should we know about you?" Mom pressed. Her simple question felt like an inquisition.

"I—I don't know," Meg stammered.

"Oh, come now," Mom coaxed. "There must be something interesting about you. You caught Lucas's attention, didn't you?"

Mom had a talent for making any statement sound like a veiled insult.

Dad was finishing off yet another drink as he blatantly checked out Meg's cleavage. Why he had to check out my date's cleavage when half the women in the room were showing a whole lot more, I didn't know. Wait… Yeah, I did know. My dad could be a real bastard. Knowing him, he'd probably bring it up later, try to bond over it or some damn thing.

If anyone ever wondered why I hated being a Prescott, this would be a prime example.

"Meg drives a motorcycle," I blurted. "It's awesome."

My parents both swiveled their heads to look at me.

"So I've heard." Mom frowned.

I glanced at Meg. She was throwing very sharp mental daggers my way.

I gave an almost imperceptible shrug. I needed my parents to take serious notice of Meg. I wanted this night to be memorable.

Reminding my parents I was dating a biker chick? *Mission accomplished.*

"I understand your dad owns a business downtown." Dad's tone implied he was less than impressed.

Meg nodded and eyed him warily.

"What kind of business?" Mom asked.

Dad waved a dismissive hand. "A little paint store."

"Do a lot of people buy paint?" Mom sounded skeptical.

"Yes, actually," Meg said firmly. "We do a lot of business with building contractors who work on hotels, apartment buildings, housing developments."

Dad gave a noncommittal grunt.

"And your mother?" Mom asked the question of Meg but she looked to Dad for the answer.

"Unemployed, I believe," Dad said. His eyebrows arched in Meg's direction. "Is that correct?"

"Oh, dear," Mom muttered, as if being unemployed were on par with being a convict. Ironic—and extremely hypocritical—considering she'd never worked a day in her life. "Unemployed."

Meg's jaw was clenched so tight it looked painful. She didn't respond to my parents' grilling. Instead she turned to me with an accusing, hurt look in her eye. She must've thought my parents had gotten the information from me.

They hadn't.

Dad had probably run a full background check on Meg the first time I mentioned her.

"You live near the downtown area?" he asked, though really, he was telling.

"Where all of those old houses are?" Mom cringed.

"Please excuse me," Meg said in a quiet, trembling voice. "I need to freshen up." She narrowed her eyes at me in a warning not to follow.

"She sounds delightful, my dear." Mom's tone was icy. I wasn't sure that Meg was out of hearing distance yet. "I wonder what Jaclyn is up to this evening."

"She's probably messing around with some guy she barely knows. It seems to be her favorite pastime." I pushed away from the table without excusing myself.

Meg was out of sight by the time I reached the massive hallway. I thought it was safe to assume she'd darted into the sanctuary of the restroom. I stood by the door for a while, waiting for her to come out.

I wasn't sure how many minutes passed. I felt as if I'd been standing there all night when I started to pace. I caught a few curious glances. I ignored them. My too-tight, absurdly shiny black dress shoes smacked against the tile as I made another pass by the ladies' room.

Chances were good there was a window in there. I wouldn't doubt Meg was angry enough to crawl through it. I continued to pace, wondering what I should do. Keep scouting out the hallway? Or maybe check the parking lot?

I spun around to make another lap when Meg exited the bathroom and crashed into my chest.

"What were you doing in there?" I demanded. "I didn't think you were ever going to come back out."

"Could you blame me?" she shot back. "That was absolutely humiliating. What did you tell your parents about me? Why did you even want me here? Did you get a kick out of them mocking my family?"

"I'm sorry. I have said very little to my parents about you. Whatever Dad found out, he found on his own. It's what he does."

"You should've warned me." Her lower lip was still trembling. I wasn't sure if it was from hurt, or anger, or possibly a combination of the two.

"You're right. I was wrong. I should've stepped in. I'm sorry for making you feel snubbed in there. For the record," I said, "there isn't another woman in that room as beautiful as you."

"Considering the amount these ladies have invested in plastic surgery, that's quite a compliment," she snarked.

"Forgive me?" I was afraid she would say no. Meg seemed tough but now that I was getting to know her, I caught glimpses of an intense vulnerability.

She crossed her arms over her chest.

I was going to have to work for it.

I took her hand in mine. My thumb traced circles on the back of her hand. "If it's any consolation, my parents are critical of *everyone*."

"Even you?"

"*Especially* me. According to them there is very little that I do right. They take every opportunity to let me know that."

"That's too bad," she said softly. "Seems to me like you're the kind of son most parents would be over the top proud of."

I noted Meg's lashes held a bit of moisture. Had my parents brought her to tears? Worse, had *I* brought her to tears with my inaction? Yet here she was, trying to make me feel better.

"You, Meg Matthews, are far more complicated than I thought."

A smile flickered across her face. "I could say the same about you. You aren't the person I thought you were. I'm glad I was wrong about you."

I couldn't think of an answer for that. In fact, I couldn't think at all. I simply acted. I leaned in and kissed her. She didn't hesitate to kiss me back. When she moaned softly and pressed her body into mine, I almost got lost in the kiss completely. My common sense yanked me back with a vengeance.

What was I *doing*? This romance was fake. But the kiss felt far too real.

Chapter Twelve

"That's it?" Francesca gave the cannoli filling a brutal stir. "He just turned around and walked away?"

"Yes." I had opened my eyes in time to see Luke's retreating back.

I swiped my finger along the side of the bowl. I popped a bit of the sweet goo into my mouth. She swatted at me, but I backed away before she made contact.

Francesca's nonna would be so proud. If she thought baking was part of the dying art of domestic abilities, my friend was always busy trying to keep it alive. Her family had been in this country for generations, and much of their cultural heritage had been lost. But food, that was the one cultural tradition they clung to.

"What did you do?" Kylie wondered.

"What *could* I do? I didn't know anyone there. By the time I got back to the table his parents were gone. I sat down and ate my crème brûlée. I ate his, too."

"And then…?" Francesca prodded.

"Just as I was thinking I might have to call one of you to ask for a ride, he showed up at the table. He said he needed a minute to pull himself together."

Francesca glanced up from her work. "I have a hard time picturing Luke falling apart in the first place."

"Right?"

"So how did you leave things?" Kylie winced, probably trying to picture herself in the situation.

"*Awkwardly*," I admitted. "He dragged me around so we could say our good-byes and then he drove me back here. He hardly said a word. It was so strange because before that I felt like we actually *connected*."

"Good-bye kiss?" Francesca wondered.

"No," I snorted an unladylike laugh. "Why would he? There was no one to show off to."

She gave me a look as she placed the cannolis on the tray. "There was no one in the hallway, either, correct?"

I moved forward and swiped some more filling. She didn't swat me away this time. "I've actually started to wonder if maybe there was. Maybe someone from school walked by— or his parents—and I didn't see them. Someone he thought was worth *persuading*." I stuffed another glob into my mouth. "I thought the kiss was a real kiss but looking back, I don't know what it was. I probably read the whole thing wrong. He was in a terrible mood after that. I felt as if I did something wrong."

"Maybe he wasn't thinking straight because of his parents," Kylie suggested.

"Definitely a possibility."

"Speaking of parents," Francesca segued a little too smoothly, "how are things going with yours?"

I made a noncommittal sound as she placed six cannolis on a small plate. I took her dirty dishes to the sink and rinsed them while she covered the larger plate and put the desserts in the fridge.

"That bad, huh?" She took the small plate and motioned for us to follow her.

We passed Mrs. Rossini as she watered the plants in the foyer. "Any left for me?" she asked.

"In the fridge," Francesca answered.

We reached her room, and she kicked the door shut. We dropped down to the floor with the plate of desserts between us.

"Talk to us," Francesca ordered. "What's going on with your parents?"

"The usual," I grudgingly admitted. "Only worse. If things don't change soon, their marriage might be over."

"Meg," Francesca said regretfully. "I'm so sorry."

"Me too," Kylie added. "Your family has been through enough the past few years."

I broke a piece off my dessert. "Can we change the subject? It's so depressing I don't even want to talk about it."

"If you decide you want to, you know we're here for you. You were both here for me last summer when Nate and I broke up."

That had been awful. He had decided he didn't want a long-distance relationship. He'd ended things at the start of the summer, and Francesca had been devastated. Apparently so was Nate, because by the time he left for college, he'd begged her to take him back.

"You're always here for me, too," Kylie added.

She was one of four girls. Her parents were overprotective to the extreme. The girl was repressed.

"Thanks. But there's not much else to say."

"You're not getting into more trouble, are you?" Francesca asked pointedly. "You haven't painted anything recently?"

When I'd requested a subject change, this was not what I

had in mind.

"No." I picked off another piece of my dessert and popped it in my mouth. Francesca would be furious if she knew I thought about it. But seeing the posters at school, hearing students murmuring about the reward, on a nearly daily basis was an *excellent* deterrent.

"Other than last night," Francesca started, "this fake relationship has been tolerable?"

"I can't believe I'm saying this, but yeah. I don't mind spending time with him."

"You seem happier than you've been in a long time." Kylie offered a relieved smile.

"Luke's a good distraction." Not only was he filling up a lot of my time, he was filling up a lot of space in my head. "He can actually be a really nice guy."

"So why don't you make the fake relationship a real relationship?" Kylie wondered.

I frowned. "That wasn't the deal."

"So change the rules."

Change the rules?

"Who says I want to?"

"Do you?" Francesca was suddenly alert.

Do I?

"I don't know. It doesn't matter because Luke said from the start he doesn't want a real relationship. That's why he's *blackmailing* me, remember?"

"That was before he got to know you." Francesca leveled a stern look at me. "I'm telling you, I've seen you together, that boy is into you."

"He's not," I corrected. "It's all for show. There's a list of rules to prove it."

"Feelings change. Look at Nate and me. We started off as friends."

"My parents are teetering on the brink of divorce. I have a

reward hanging over my head. Getting emotionally involved with someone is the last thing I need," I decided. "Luke and I are friends, nothing more."

"Then you can't let him get away with kissing you like that." Francesca scowled, indignant on my behalf. "He's taking advantage of the situation."

"Unless you *want* him to kiss you like that." Kylie made a dreamy face. "He's so cute. I know I would kiss that boy every chance I got."

I grinned. "I didn't exactly mind."

"So you *do* have feelings for him," Francesca pressed.

"I didn't say *that*," I corrected. "I just said kissing him is… not terrible. I mean, the only guy I've ever dated was Gavin." Gavin McKenzie and I'd dated for three whopping months freshman year before he moved away. It was just as well, because Sydney's diagnosis soon followed. "Kissing Gavin was nothing like kissing Luke."

"I suppose not," Francesca said wryly. "Just don't lose sight of what's really going on."

"I won't." I hesitated. "I'm tired of being miserable all the time. High school is almost over. I feel like it passed in this awful, dark haze. I'm stuck with Luke for now. I can either mope around about it or I can try to enjoy it."

"Be careful, Meg," Francesca warned. "Don't let yourself enjoy it *too* much."

• • •

"Nutmeg."

I nearly ran into a tree as I swiveled my head around to look over my shoulder. I skidded to a stop as Luke jogged up the trail, closing the distance between us.

Lady yipped in greeting.

"Hey, there," Luke said. "You must be Lady." He knelt

and held out his hand. She sniffed it and then plopped onto her haunches. Her tongue lolled as he gave her a good rub down. After a few minutes he returned his attention to me.

"I didn't know you were a runner."

"I'm more of a slow jogger," I admitted. "Lady starts out with a lot of energy, but she loses momentum pretty quickly."

"Mind if I join you?"

"You won't get much of a run in," I warned. I took off at our usual plodding pace. Luke slowed his stride to match ours.

The trail was narrow, barely wide enough for two people to run side by side. Trees flanked the edges. It wound through the woods, curving around the park.

The sound of our feet smacking the packed dirt and Lady's panting filled my ears, and I suddenly felt awkward. I couldn't think of anything to say that wouldn't make it worse. His behavior after the kiss left me mentally floundering.

I was grateful that he'd caught up to us so late. The trail would be spilling us back into the park soon.

He was the one to break our silence. "You're mad about last night."

"I'm not mad. I'm confused," I confessed.

"I was going to call you tonight so we could talk about it. Since we're both here, I guess we should talk about it now."

"So talk."

"I wanted to apologize again for the way my parents treated you. For the way I let them treat you."

"Apology accepted."

"And the kiss," he blurted. "I should apologize for that, too. Emotions were running pretty high. I guess we kind of got caught up in the moment. I did, anyway."

"Is that what happened?"

"Isn't it?" His tone was guarded, making me feel as if I needed to answer carefully.

"I don't know. *You* kissed *me*." Never mind that I didn't

resist. Resist? I practically melted all over him.

The trail widened, and we jogged onto an open field. I could see Luke's SUV parked at the edge of it. We slowed our pace to a walk. He headed that way and I reflexively followed.

"You're not really my girlfriend."

"Yes, Luke, I'm aware." Irritation flooded my words. "I have not forgotten you're blackmailing me."

He gave me a scolding look. "What I'm trying to say is that I know I can't just kiss you for the hell of it. That wasn't the agreement. It won't happen again."

"Is that why you disappeared after?"

"Yeah." He gave me a sheepish smile. "I felt like an ass."

We reached his Navigator. "As long as you're here," he said, "I've got something to show you."

Lady sprawled out on the asphalt as I waited for Luke.

"This will just take a second." He pulled something out of his backseat.

The notebook, of course. It was opened to the list. He held it up for me to see. The whole page had become a mish-mash of scribbles. His precise script, my sloppy loops, different colored pens, pencils…and now a sentence highlighted in yellow.

Luke will defend Meg, especially when it comes to his crazy-ass parents.

"I added it as soon as I got home."

"You highlighted it, even." For some reason, I found that amusing and oddly endearing.

"I'm taking that rule very seriously from now on."

Lady whined. She was probably thirsty.

"I'm hungry," Luke said after shooting her a glance. "We could go get burgers and onion rings. I'll even throw in a burger for the fur ball. You hungry?"

"Starving. But as you pointed out earlier, I'm not really

your girlfriend. I'll eat at home." I kept my tone light, but Francesca's warning buzzed in my head. I could enjoy my time with Luke, but I needed to remember what this was really about. "I think I've maxed out my quota for the amount of time I'm required to spend with you this week." I backed up. Lady got to her feet. "See you at school."

I took off at a jog and he didn't try to stop me.

The television murmured quietly in the living room when I got home. A quick peek around the corner let me know both my parents were here. At least they weren't avoiding each other. They were simply ignoring each other. I trudged up the staircase.

When I changed out of my running clothes, I paused for a moment to straighten the pictures wedged into my mirror. My gaze rested on a photo of Sydney and me building a sand castle at the coast.

I could finally remember that day with a smile. Miss Perez had told me time would heal. I had clung to that promise like a lifeline. Slowly, I'd been able to pull myself out of the abyss of blackness.

These days I tried to concentrate on the time I'd had with her. Not the time that was lost.

Lady whimpered, as if she knew where my thoughts had gone. I knelt down. She pressed against me, giving me a doggy hug.

"You miss her, too, don't you?"

Her absence would always be felt.

As a family we spent years readjusting our lives to meet Sydney's needs. We gave up our house. Mom gave up her job. Dad started working at the store more, no longer able to afford to pay an employee.

I'd had to give up sports when my parents no longer had the time to take me, or the money to invest in me.

Other than hanging onto Francesca and Kylie, I'd given

up any semblance of a social life. I'd wanted to spend every moment I could with my sister. We knew her days were numbered. I hadn't wanted to miss any of them.

Everything revolved around Sydney.

Somewhere along the way I'd lost myself.

I didn't realize I still hadn't gotten myself back until Luke started pressing me. He'd asked about my hobbies, my interests. Maybe it was time to look for something that would make *me* happy.

Even if I didn't know what that was anymore.

Chapter Thirteen

"Close the refrigerator," Mom ordered. "You're going to ruin your appetite."

"Mom. When have I *ever* ruined my appetite?"

Ignoring the question, she said, "Go upstairs and change into something decent. The Winterses will be here shortly."

I nabbed a handful of cookies out of the cupboard before her words hit me. "Wait. What?"

"Dinner. Tonight. With the Winterses."

"Can't make it." No wonder the kitchen smelled like an Italian restaurant. My stomach rumbled, but I wasn't going to stick around to see what Mom had in the oven.

"Luke."

I stopped at the foot of the stairs.

Mom wore her stubborn face. "You will be here."

"I have plans." Plans that I'd just conjured up in the last sixty seconds, but still, they were plans.

"I told you about this."

"Nope. Pretty sure you didn't. I would've remembered. You trying to shove Jaclyn at me isn't something I'd forget. Thanks for the warning though, I appreciate it."

"You're being rude. When are you going to stop behaving like such a child?" she scolded. "This dinner isn't about you. You know your father and I enjoy George and Eileen's company. We always have."

"Perfect. Since this isn't about me and you enjoy their company *so* much, there's no reason for me to stay."

"What am I supposed to tell them?"

"Tell them I have a date with my girlfriend."

Her face twisted into a look of irritation. It was a look that said *Just wait until your father gets home.*

I wasn't stupid enough to do that. I darted up the staircase, grabbed my phone and a few other essentials, and within minutes I was tearing out of the driveway.

I made a phone call, made a pit stop, and an hour later Meg and I were watching the waves roll in at the coast.

I called her, obviously very last minute. But the moment I mentioned the word "ocean" she was all in.

I shook out the green blanket that resided in the back of my SUV. Once we got settled I dug in my cooler and passed her a root beer before divvying up the food I'd picked up at the deli.

"I haven't been here in forever," she said. She wore a faraway look as she gazed out at the water. Too often I caught a glimpse of something dark behind her eyes. A sadness lingering right below the surface.

I got the impression there was a lot more to this girl than I'd first thought. At times I wanted to ask her about it. Common sense told me she wouldn't appreciate it. Wouldn't answer. It would do no good to ask.

"We hit a good day." Soon the rainy season would begin, and the weather would cool off.

"What's the deal with the baseball bats that were in your backseat? Those weren't really all yours, were they?"

"That's a random question."

She shrugged. "Not really. I'm curious."

The bats, the ones she'd automatically assumed were all for me. Because I was some spoiled rich kid. I hadn't corrected her at the time because I'd told myself I didn't care what she thought.

Apparently I cared now, whether I wanted to or not.

"They weren't mine," I confirmed. "I worked for a community project last summer. It focused on getting at-risk kids involved in sports. It was aimed at all sports but it's not exactly a secret that I have a soft spot for baseball. I took my earnings and bought the bats with it. The sports shop in town gave me a discount because I ordered in bulk. The order had just come in, and I hadn't had a chance to drop them off with the program director yet."

"I heard a rumor that you might also be responsible for a large donation of equipment last summer." Her tone held a hint of approval.

"A rumor? Did Nate pass that along?" She nodded. "The program is through a non-profit organization. Dad can be generous when something is a tax write-off. I've learned to make something sound as if it's in his best interest." Even then, I'd had to work for it.

"But the bats you bought yourself."

"I obviously didn't take the job for the money."

"Why did you get involved, then?"

"Right now, baseball is just about the most important thing to me."

She cocked her head to the side. "Why? It's just a sport."

"Not to me it's not. What's with all the questions?"

"It's called conversation." She threw a piece of crust at me. It bounced off my shoulder and instantly became a seagull snack. "Why is baseball so important to you? Are you planning on going pro? I've heard you're good enough."

"I'm good, but not that good. But baseball, it's my way out." The only way out I could think of.

"Your way out of where?"

"Out from under my dad's thumb. He's got my life mapped out. Ivy League college, then joining him at his law firm. It was the same for my brother. Now Gabe is miserable. He has a wife and a newborn baby girl he almost never sees. Dad sends him all over the country, has him work hours no human should have to work. He drives the car Dad wants him to drive, lives in the house Dad thinks he should live in. Dad controls his salary, his bonuses, where he's going to be just about every hour of every damn day. I don't want that. And that's not even the worst of it."

Once there was a crack in the dam storing my thoughts on the matter, I couldn't stop them from dumping out.

"I don't want to be a lawyer. I sure as hell don't want to be a lawyer in his firm. Don't even get me started on some of those bastards he represents. I couldn't live with myself if I helped some of these corporations get away with doing the things they've done." I dragged a hand through my hair. "Sorry. That was a little too much information."

She smiled. "I like getting to know you better."

As soon as we finished eating, Meg began scavenging for a stick. When she found what she was looking for, she took off toward the beach. I was curious enough to follow.

She began to swirl out lazy doodles and squiggles. The ocean crashed behind her, with the sun falling low on the horizon. The breeze toyed with her hair. I found myself wishing I was the one toying with that amazing hair.

Totally not allowed.

"Tell me something I don't know about you."

She paused with the stick in her hand. "Why?"

"It would make me feel better. I practically bared my soul to you just now," I said, keeping my tone light.

Her brow furrowed as she set to work again. "You asked before about my parents letting me ride a motorcycle. What I didn't say was that I'd been riding it for a few months before they found out."

"You snuck it out of the garage."

She nodded. "When Dad caught me, he was pretty mad. I was grounded for weeks. Eventually I wore him down and convinced him I respected the machine and knew how to be safe."

"Wore him down?"

"I'm not proud to say I may have used a guilt trip or two."

I glanced down and realized she'd just etched the image from her mural. Before I could ask about it, she was questioning me again.

"How is baseball your way out? You said you aren't good enough to go pro."

I was treading awfully close to a truth I couldn't admit to. It didn't stop me from spilling my guts anyway.

"Because if I don't do what Dad wants me to do, he'll cut me off financially. I should've spent my entire high school baseball career working on getting noticed by scouts. Now we've started senior year. I'm in a time crunch and playing catch-up. There's a camp in Colorado over Christmas break. It could be my *one* chance to get noticed. There's going to be scouts from a dozen or more universities. Some of these guys have been making a name for themselves for years, but it was only the last year or so that I realized baseball might be my ticket out. I have a good shot at a scholarship if I can just prove myself."

"And if you don't get a scholarship, you could always pay for college yourself. Lots of people do."

"Pay for college myself?" I blurted. "How the hell am I

supposed to do that?"

"Chances are, I'm going to end up with student loans."

"Loans? I'd be paying off my education for years." I was overwhelmed by the idea. But was it any worse than the alternative?

She rolled her eyes and whipped her stick into the ocean. "Welcome to how the other half lives."

• • •

"Lucas."

I clomped into the parlor. My parents and Jaclyn's were sitting around, drinks in hand. All eyes turned to me when I entered. I gave the polite greeting I knew was expected. I felt a momentary burst of relief that Jaclyn was absent.

"I hope you had a good evening." Mom's tone was a contradiction to her words. "It would've been nice if you were home sooner. Jaclyn could've used your company."

"Better late than never," Eileen chirped. "I hope you don't mind but your mother said she could watch television in your room. Our conversation bores her."

My room? As if there weren't half a dozen other TVs in the house.

I shot Mom a pissed-off glare, not caring who else saw, before storming up the stairs.

"Miss me?" Jaclyn cooed when I barged in.

The sight of her lounging on my sofa—bare feet on my coffee table while she watched some lame reality show—made my blood sizzle.

"Nope," I tossed back. "Get out."

"What's the matter, Luke? Afraid I'm going to spill your secret?"

My eyes darted around. I hated that she'd been in here alone. Not that there was anything to find. My backpack—

with the rules—was in my Navigator. My stomach twisted, knowing how smug she'd be. Jaclyn wasn't book smart. But she was a world-class conniver. If she'd found anything, she'd have me on my knees already, begging for mercy.

She picked up my brand new copy of *Cather in the Rye*. "You are such a closet geek."

"Whatever. Just leave."

"I don't want to." She wiggled her manicured toes.

I stared her down.

She got to her feet, moving like a cat ready to pounce on a stupid, unsuspecting mouse. I took a step toward the door when she closed the distance between us.

"Haven't you punished me long enough?" she pouted.

"I don't know what you're talking about."

"Oh, please." She rolled her eyes and her voice became harsh. "Meg? Seriously? I'm not buying it. You're pissed at me. So you decide to date the trashiest girl you can find? Fine. Yes. It's *humiliating* that you have everyone thinking you prefer her. Isn't that what you want, to make me look bad?"

"My life doesn't revolve around you."

"It should," she purred. She reached for my cheek. I swatted her hand away. "We're good together. You know we are."

I was going to get whiplash from her constantly changing attitude.

"I don't think so." I laughed.

Frustration rippled below her artfully made up face. "You run around, have your fun. I can take it. But sooner or later, you're going to come to your senses. We could be the sort of power couple that would put our parents to shame one day."

"You're crazy."

"I'm *right*." Her eyes dug into me. "Meg's not good enough for you. Her dad owns a paint store. Her mother does nothing."

"How do you know that?" I regretted the question instantly.

She flashed a wicked smile. "I'm resourceful. You'd be surprised at what I know."

I had no idea if she was bluffing.

"Everyone has secrets, Luke."

"Even you?" I taunted. "I mean, other than you hop into bed with any guy who makes you see dollar signs? Then again, that's not much of a secret. Oh. Wait. I bet your prim and proper mother doesn't know."

"Do you think Meg's any different?"

"I'm not discussing Meg with you." I stepped out into the hallway. "Coming?" I didn't wait for an answer. I knew she'd follow. She had to keep up appearances. It would look bad to her daddy if she sequestered herself away while I joined them.

I hadn't even reached the staircase before Jaclyn scampered up behind me. I was choosing the lesser of two evils. Hang out downstairs with the parents, or hang out alone in my room with Jaclyn.

Parents won out. Obviously.

Chapter Fourteen

MEG

Well over a month into our arrangement, things were starting to feel oddly…normal. As the weather turned cooler I was becoming accustomed to hopping into Luke's nice, warm SUV every morning. The temptation to let him pick me up instead of riding my Rebel was increasing with each blustery day. But I hadn't succumbed yet.

Jaclyn was still with Trevor. I had started to wonder if maybe he had grown on her. She barely paid any attention to Luke at all anymore, which is exactly what he had wanted.

I knew when this was over it would leave an enormous blank space in my life.

I tried not to think about it.

For now, I was enjoying myself.

Most days. Today was not one of those days.

"This goes above and beyond," I whispered to Luke as he took my hand. He led me through the door of Natalia's.

The hostess led us to a private back room. Luke's parents

were already seated.

"Happy birthday, Mrs. Prescott." I forced a smile onto my face.

"Thank you." She eyed me up like I was a fly in her merlot.

"Nice of you to finally join us," she said to Luke.

"Sorry," he replied. "Dad didn't give me much warning, but he insisted I needed to invite Meg."

"Did he?" She turned her attention from Luke to raise a questioning brow at her husband.

"I thought we ought to get to know her a little better," Edward explained.

"If you were going to invite guests, I really would've preferred that you invite the Winterses," she scolded. "It's been too long since we've seen them."

"The waiter should be back shortly," Edward told us, ignoring his wife. His menu was already resting in front of him, as was Lenore's. An open bottle of wine sat between them. Their glasses were already more than half empty.

I picked up my menu and started flipping through it. I was scanning the pastas when our waiter returned.

"Do you know what you're having?" Luke asked.

"The crab ravioli."

"Are you sure?" Mr. Prescott frowned.

Was it too expensive? I tried to find something in the lower range because I didn't want him to think I was taking advantage of him. Ravioli wasn't exceptionally high priced. Not like the *Risotto Pescatore* or the *Zuppa Di Pesce*.

"Would you prefer that I order something else?"

"It's just that there are an awful lot of calories in that. And if you add in a bit of bread you'll be on carbohydrate overload. You've got some nice curves now but it doesn't take much to turn curves into—"

"Dad!" Luke shot me an apologetic look.

I wanted to tell him he had nothing to be sorry for. If

anything, *I* felt sorry for *him*. My parents had flaws but at least they had manners. "It's fine," I assured him, wanting to keep the peace. I quickly rewound my memory. Lenore had ordered a Caesar salad, dressing on the side "I'll have a Caesar salad as well. Dressing on the side."

Edward nodded his approval.

I almost wished I'd ordered the ravioli out of spite. Edward was one of the last people I wanted to impress. But if it would ease tensions between him and Luke, I was willing to play into this nonsense for one night.

The waiter scribbled my order onto his pad, asked if we needed anything else, and then hurried away.

"You know who has a great figure?" Edward unfurled his cloth napkin with a flourish.

"Dad," Luke said in a warning tone.

"Jaclyn," Edward declared. "That's who."

I didn't even try to suppress my grimace. Was he trying to embarrass me? If so, it wasn't working. I couldn't stop thinking *he* should be embarrassed. What kind of father checks out his son's girlfriend? *Ewww.*

"That girl is simply lovely," Lenore agreed.

Dinner was a progression of refilled wineglasses and backhanded compliments. Every now and again, an outright insult would be flung. Edward and Lenore made no effort to pull me into the conversation. I was okay with that. The less attention they paid to me, the better. It was a perk of a fake relationship. I had no desire to impress his parents.

"Isn't Gabe supposed to be here?" Luke finally asked. "I wanted him to meet Meg."

"I'd love to meet your brother," I said. It had become clear to me that Luke and Gabe were close. I had a hunch they were a lot alike.

His mother gave us a tight smile. "He's not here because Edward sent him to New York for the weekend."

"He went to New York because he knows what it takes to get things done," Edward corrected. He pointed at Luke. "You could learn a lot from him. In fact, you could start by concentrating a bit more on your schoolwork."

"Dad," he said firmly, "I'm not quitting baseball."

I hadn't realized there was a threat in his words, but Luke had read between the lines just fine.

"I think you ought to concentrate a little more on your GPA and a little less on your extracurricular," Edward reprimanded.

"You told me that as long as I keep my GPA where you want it, I could play. I've done that," Luke said.

"I bet you could raise it even more if you applied yourself," Edward argued.

"Luke studies all the time," I interjected. He was holding his own, but I felt the need to defend him. "His grades are excellent."

"There's always room for improvement," Edward pressed.

Was this what it was like to have a lawyer for a parent?

Luke gave me a strained smile before returning his attention to Edward.

"Dad, you know as well as I do that Ivy Leagues are going to be looking at extra-curricular activities as well as grades. It's definitely in my best interest to play."

"All I'm saying is you need to keep your eyes on the future, son. There's a lot of planning and forethought that goes into success."

"Your father and I have tried to set you up for it as best as we can, but you seem intent on fighting us every step of the way." Lenore's cool gaze chilled me as she spoke. "Tell us, Meg, what are your plans for after high school?"

I shifted in my seat, wishing I'd kept quiet, continuing to go unnoticed. It was too late for that as they both stared at me, waiting for a response.

"I'd like to be a guidance counselor."

"You mean at a *school*?" She grimaced in distaste, as if I'd admitted I had aspirations of becoming an armed robber.

"Yes, at a school." I wanted to hold her gaze, but I felt myself wavering under her scrutiny.

Her face puckered. "Why?"

"Why not?" Luke inserted.

"Jaclyn—"

"Stop." Luke slapped his napkin down on the table. "Stop trying to shove Jaclyn and me together." He spoke his next words slowly. "It's never going to happen."

Lenore blinked in surprise while Edward guzzled more wine.

My heart went out to Luke. For the first time I understood why he would go to a level as desperate as blackmail. Even with me—his supposed girlfriend—sitting *right here*, his parents wouldn't let up. Or maybe it was *because* I was here. I got the distinct impression Lenore was trying to make me uncomfortable.

I was uncomfortable, but not in the way I suspected she wanted. The more his parents talked, the less I respected them. How did Luke deal with this on a regular basis?

"Do you really think she's that perfect for me?" he demanded. "Or is this about you and Dad needing to control *everything* in my life?"

"Yes," Lenore said firmly, "I do think Jaclyn is an exceptional young woman. I also think you're veering onto a dangerous path. As your parents it's our duty to steer you back in the direction you belong."

"Mom," his voice shook with anger, "she cheated on me. A lot."

She did? He'd never mentioned that before. I hadn't exactly asked. He spoke with anger, but hurt laced his tone as well.

Lenore waved her hand, as if whisking such nonsense away.

"I tracked her down. Believe me, you do not want the details of what I walked in on."

Lenore frowned. "Eileen recently told me Jaclyn confided in her. She said this scenario was the other way around." Her eyes raked over me with a burning hatred. "Jaclyn confessed she found you in a compromising position with…*someone*."

Me? My partially eaten salad wanted to stage a revolt.

Luke pushed his chair back as he stood. "You and Eileen better get your facts straight. Jaclyn's an expert at lying and scheming, twisting everything around to benefit herself. If you believe her, over me, we've got a real problem. Why don't you check the surveillance tapes from the entryway of the firm? You know where Jaclyn likes to go? Her dad's office after hours. It's nice and private and perfect for…entertaining."

I scampered after him as he hurried out of the restaurant.

He was silent as we drove away. I let him simmer. For a while he just drove aimlessly around the edges of town. By the time we turned into his driveway his tension had eased.

I didn't care to witness a repeat of the evening.

"Are you sure you want to be here?" I asked. "I thought you'd rather avoid your parents for a while."

"They won't be home. Did you see the limo outside of Natalia's? Dad's taking Mom to Sapphire Bay for the night. They won't be back until tomorrow." He parked but turned to me before cutting the engine. "Do *you* want to be here? We can do something else."

He looked like he could use a friend.

"We can hang out here."

He grimaced. "My Dad had no right commenting on your curves, which *I* think are amazing, by the way. But I've learned when he gets like that, the fastest way to shut him down is by not engaging."

"I get it." I did. The last thing I wanted was to hear Luke and his Dad arguing about my body. I couldn't imagine anything more awkward.

As soon as we were inside he seemed more relaxed. "I'm glad you decided to stay. I have something for you."

"Is it something shiny?"

He laughed. "No."

"Is it a pony?"

Still laughing he said, "No. Do you want a pony?"

"Not necessarily." I just wanted to lighten the mood.

He grabbed my hand and led me to the back staircase. I was a little surprised we weren't going to his room. At the bottom of the steps he tugged me down a hallway, then pushed open the first door on the left and flipped on the light.

There were no windows. The walls were painted burgundy, the carpet charcoal gray. Movie posters were framed and lined three of the walls. The fourth held an enormous screen. The floor was tiered, three levels, and each housed a long, plush sofa.

The room wasn't massive, just perfect for a small group. A retro popcorn maker stood against one wall, a small fridge next to it. The scent of buttered popcorn from days past lingered in the air. A rack of movies lined another wall.

"This is amazing. Why haven't we used this room before?"

A sweet smile danced on his lips. "I was saving it for a rainy day."

"A rainy day?"

He moved to the massive rack that held the movies. Twisting around he held up *Breakfast at Tiffany's*. "You said you love watching black and white movies on a rainy day. It's not raining, but maybe we could watch it anyway. I bought several, so if you'd rather watch something else…"

"No," I said. "That one is perfect. Thank you." I surprised us both by sliding my arms around him.

"You're welcome," he said as he hugged me back.

We stood like that for a few moments, neither of us coming up with anything to say...but neither of us really seeming to want to break away.

"We should put the movie in," I finally said.

"On it."

I scanned the other titles while I waited. I hadn't realized how many movies I'd missed when my life had been in an upheaval.

"Top row is the best." He led me to my seat. I settled in, and he reached for a remote. With one button he turned off the lights. With the other he turned up the volume. I hadn't noticed the speakers, but the surround sound kicked in as the movie began. It was like being in a real theater, only the intimacy made it a whole lot better. The couch was so plush it was like sitting on a cushion of cotton candy.

He set the remote on the floor near his feet. He looped an arm around my shoulders, tucking me into his side. His hand rested on my arm, his fingers lazily tracing nonsensical shapes.

How could a simple brushing of fingers feel so good? How could it make my skin sizzle? With every seemingly thoughtless stroke, my insides liquefied.

I wasn't exactly sure when being blackmailed had become so enjoyable. Luke wasn't anything like I thought he would be. He was constantly making small, sweet gestures. He'd far too easily won me over.

His parents were gone almost every weekend. We spent a lot of time at his house. But I had given up hope of digging up dirt on him. To be honest, even if I found something, I wasn't sure I'd use it. I was past that.

As his warm body pressed against mine, I felt myself melting against his side. I placed one hand against his abs and fought the urge to let my fingers slide under his shirt.

The preview clips ended and our movie started. I only

vaguely noticed. I was completely consumed by Luke's presence. Totally aware that I was feeling things I shouldn't be feeling.

I was also aware that there was no reason—no real reason at all—for him to be playing the loving boyfriend.

That didn't stop Luke from continuing to trace a trail up and down my bare arm. I turned to steal a glance at him but when I did, I realized he was already watching me. The soft glow of the movie screen flickered across his face, and when I looked at him, he didn't look away. His face was close to mine. His lips only inches away. I realized I was staring at them.

It was stupid of me, I knew. There should be no kissing. There was no reason for it. But that didn't stop him from leaning in. That didn't stop my eyes from fluttering shut. That didn't stop us from kissing anyway.

Chapter Fifteen

Luke

Rain was pouring from the sky in relentless sheets. My wipers couldn't keep up; the outside world was a blur. I pulled over to the curb a few doors down from the little pale blue house I knew was Meg's. I'd checked it out one time, out of fake-boyfriend obligation. I had thought more than once it would put me into accidental-stalker territory.

Thunder rumbled, shaking my SUV.

From here I'd be able to see Meg if she left. No way would I allow her to ride her Rebel in this weather. I wasn't sure what she did on rainy days. Maybe one of her friends picked her up. I didn't call ahead because I figured she'd tell me to stay away.

Silence filled the air as I watched lightning dart across the sky. My hands strummed relentlessly against the steering wheel.

At the park, I'd told Meg I was going to watch myself. I'd promised her I wouldn't be crossing lines that shouldn't be crossed.

Yeah, we'd crossed a few lines together the other night. But I still felt responsible. This whole scheme was my idea. In my own way, I had as much riding on it as she did.

I wasn't looking forward to the conversation we were about to have.

Meg stepped onto her front porch. She stood under the overhang, looking tense, as if she were about to dart into the rain. I coasted down the block as I gave my horn a tap.

I was violating the fake boyfriend code by being here, breaking a rule she'd underlined. I expected her to scowl, maybe even ignore me and dart into the rain anyway. But when her lips tilted and her eyebrow quirked, I knew I wouldn't be in too much trouble.

I pulled into her driveway, edging as close to the porch as I could get. She leapt off the steps and yanked open the passenger door, then scrambled inside and turned to face me.

"What are you doing here?"

I reached for my secret weapon. Holding up the white bakery bag I said, "Bringing you breakfast. And keeping you dry."

She sniffed the air before tugging the bag out of my hand. Her eyes lit up when she pulled out the chocolate croissant. I'd learned Meg had a constant craving for onion rings and baked goods. Not necessarily together. And it was way too early for onion rings.

I motioned to the cup holder. "And an extra large hot chocolate."

I figured I was in the clear so I started backing out of the driveway. I caught a glimpse of Meg's mom standing at the kitchen window. Meg lifted her hand tentatively and waved. Her mom waved back, and then we were cruising down the street.

"Is that going to be a problem?" I asked.

"I doubt it. Mom doesn't exactly give a lot of thought to

what I do. Still. You're not supposed to be here, you know," she scolded.

I dared a glance her way. "I couldn't let you ride in the rain."

"I would never ride in a storm like this." She grimaced. "I was contemplating taking the bus. Or borrowing Mom's minivan. I guess I owe you a thank-you because you saved me from having to decide which form of humiliation I preferred."

She moaned as she took a bite of her croissant. Her eyes were closed as she leaned her head against the seat. She looked completely blissed-out. I was lucky I didn't jump the curb as I struggled to keep my eyes off her.

"Did you see the weather forecast?" A lame topic, for sure, but I needed to get my head on straight. "It looks like the rainy season has officially hit. Maybe I should pick you up every day."

"Maybe you should."

"What? No argument? What's going on here?"

"I'm choosing a ride with you over taking Mom's rusted-up minivan. That's not something to get too cocky about." Her tone was light, taking any sting out of her words.

She took another bite of her breakfast, sighing in appreciation this time. I kept my mouth shut and drove.

"You know, you're really not so bad," she teased.

"I'm sorry," I leaned closer, "I didn't hear you. Could you repeat that?"

She laughed as she nudged me away. "Stop or I won't share my croissant with you."

"That's okay. I already ate two."

We pulled into the parking lot. A few kids were hanging out in their cars, but it looked like most had already headed inside. It didn't look as if the storm was going to lighten up anytime soon.

"Here's your rainy day," Meg said.

"Yeah. I noticed it showed up a few days too late." I

clenched the steering wheel. "About the other night…"

She looked at me over the edge of her cup.

"I'm—"

She groaned, cutting me off. "Please do not say you're sorry for kissing me again."

"You said from the start no kissing unless necessary."

"And you said from the start we should try to have a little bit of fun."

Right. I did say that. That wasn't exactly what I'd meant by fun. Mostly because I didn't think she'd be open to it.

"You made it perfectly clear you didn't want a real relationship," she reminded.

"So the other night was…?"

"Fun." Her face contorted into a look of uncertainty. "Unless it wasn't, um, fun for you? If it wasn't, I totally get it. I know I'm not exactly your type. I guess I just assumed that you liked kissing me. Since we did a lot of it."

I wasn't sure that "fun" was entirely fitting. I could think of a few other words to describe the other night more accurately. But I knew what she was getting at.

"I had a lot of…*fun.*"

"Perfect. Then I don't see a problem. Do you?"

"You're serious?" This was not how I thought this conversation was going to go.

She lowered her gaze as she twisted the cup around in her hands. I *knew* she was going to have second thoughts. I waited for them to come but she surprised me again.

"Let's just say you're not the only one with majorly messed up parents. I know you've promised not to tell, but every day I hear people gossiping about my mural. The principal mentions the reward during every Monday morning announcement. I feel this weight hanging over me. I'm just waiting for it to fall and crush me." She lifted her gaze to mine again. "It just felt *really* good to get out of my own head for a while. You know?"

"You've had a front row seat to my crazy family. So yeah, I do know. But just to be sure we're on the same page, you're talking no strings attached?" I had to clarify. Had to for both of us. For reasons I could never explain to her, this *relationship*…or whatever it was…could only go so far.

"No strings that aren't already tied to the rules."

"So you were using me?" I teased. "To get out of your own head."

Her eyebrows lifted. "Did you mind?"

"Not. At. All."

"I guess there's only one thing to do then."

I wasn't sure I was totally buying it, but wasn't opposed to giving it a go.

"Make out?" I asked hopefully.

She laughed as she went for the notebook. She made two quick slashes across the page.

I stopped her before she tossed it over the seat.

"That was fast. Let me see."

She held it up.

Luke ~~cannot~~ kiss Meg whenever he wants.

"You can add that it works both ways."

"I'll make a mental note of it." The notebook landed in the back with a little thump.

Next thing I knew, we were kissing again. Definitely one of my favorite ways to start the day. We jumped apart when Adam pounded on my hood as he walked by, alerting us to the fact it was time to go.

"Stay put a second." I grabbed the umbrella I'd thought to toss in my backseat. I hurried around to her door so she could slide under it.

"Thanks for breakfast," she said as we ran though the rain. "Just please don't make it a daily thing. I don't think my jeans could handle it."

I thought her curves could handle it just fine.

"I do have a favor to ask," I said.

"Name it."

We tromped up the steps.

"Leo is having a party on Saturday." I pulled one of the doors open. As soon as we were in the entryway I folded in the umbrella. We were alone for the moment.

"Saturday? Saturday is a bad day for me."

"Do you work?"

She hesitantly shook her head and began to fidget with the straps of her bag. "No. But I have other obligations."

I waited for her to elaborate. She remained silent as she shuffled her feet and refused to look at me. This party was important. My teammates would be there. They would all have dates. This was exactly the sort of thing I needed her for. Plus, I realized I also wanted her there. I liked having her around.

"Why not?" I demanded.

"I…have plans."

I studied her face. "That didn't sound very convincing."

"I have plans," she said more firmly. "Saturday won't work for me."

"Make it work," I ordered.

Her jaw clenched, and her eyes flashed. I remembered how well ordering her to go to the ball had worked out. I instantly backtracked. "Please," I said with a bit less force, "make it work. Rearrange your schedule or something."

"I can't." She looked past me, studying the reward poster on the wall.

I scoffed in frustration. "Why not? This is important to me, Meg."

"I thought it was just a party. How important can it be?"

"For years Leo's family has thrown a big bash for the baseball players. They did it for his four brothers, and now him. It's a way to stay connected during the off-season. It's tradition."

"I'm sure you're perfectly capable of having a good time without me."

I shook my head. "I won't."

"Oh my gosh," she groaned. "You're *pouting*."

"I'm not pouting." I was getting pissed. Her shift in attitude had me on high alert. She wouldn't look at me, wouldn't answer me. It was a total Jaclyn move. I felt like I was being jerked around. "Do you have a date or something?"

"Are you kidding me right now?"

She looked at me with big, sad eyes. I felt my frustration fizzle.

"Look," I tried again, "I need you to go to this. Okay? It'll look bad if you don't. Everyone is going to ask where you are. It's kind of a big deal to me."

"Tell them I'm busy."

"Doing what?"

"I have a prior obligation."

"So you've claimed. But you haven't told me what you're doing." Suspicion tore at my insides. How did I know for sure she wasn't hooking up with another guy? Not that I was jealous. It just wasn't allowed.

It wasn't a written rule but it was implied.

"Maybe," she said with an edge to her tone, "that's because it's none of your business."

"Fine," I growled. "I'll let you off this time, but you need to remember that you owe me."

"As if you'd ever let me forget it." she shot back.

I yanked one of the double doors open, and Meg stomped through them.

This morning had turned into a roller coaster, throwing me one loop after another.

Chapter Sixteen

MEG

My hair whipped around my face as it was tugged loose from its ponytail. The day was dreary but so far the rain had held off. The wind coming off the ocean had a bite to it, the kind that took hold of you and burrowed down into your bones. My leather pants and jacket did only so much to keep me warm.

The waves crashed in front of me, the outcropping of rocks rising up behind me. This was my sister's favorite place back when she was well enough to leave the house. I sank down onto a smooth ledge. It was more secluded here than the popular, sandy strips of beach.

I had visited the cemetery earlier out of a sense of obligation but hadn't stayed long. I didn't feel close to her there. Not like I did here. Sydney would sit at this beach for hours with her sketchpad, watching the ocean, listening to the waves, trying to capture the multihued sunsets. When I wanted to remember Sydney, and truly feel close to her, this is where I came.

This was where we spent the day before her test results came back. I think my parents were expecting the worst. I think they brought us here, hoping for one last, carefree day as a family before our world crumbled. We made sandcastles, had a picnic, flew kites.

Closing my eyes, it was easy to picture my sister. The sunshine on her cheeks, a smile on her lips. Her chin-length red hair would whip around her face. On windy days, her delicate body looked as if it might blow away.

Not for the first time I wondered what Sydney would think of my tributes to her. Would she adore them? Be worried? Fearful I would get caught?

I hadn't painted a single mural since the night Luke caught me. Sitting here reminded me of why I'd started painting the murals in the first place. Would it really be so bad if I added just one more to my repertoire? As thoughts of my sister spilled through my mind, it was easy to justify my actions.

At least to myself.

Today was the anniversary I'd been dreading. Today, one year ago, was the day we'd lost her. She never made it to thirteen.

I tried to mentally sidestep those memories. I wanted to remember the good things. I wanted to honor Sydney today by remembering her life, not by dwelling on her death.

Today was a day we should be remembering her as a family.

Instead Dad had left for work before the sun had risen. Mom had started the day in Sydney's room with the door closed. The silence of our house had been punctuated by tortured sobs. I had only been able to take so much.

I had ignored calls from both Kylie and Francesca.

When I couldn't take listening to Mom's heartbreak anymore, I'd taken off.

Eventually a sense of duty won over. I realized that today, of all days, Mom might need me as much as I needed her.

When I rolled into my driveway, Luke's empty Navigator was the last thing I expected to see. I stormed into the house. Mom was on the sofa, a Hallmark movie on—though I doubted she was actually watching it—a box of tissues rested next to her.

Her expression was nearly devoid of emotion. She didn't even turn to me when I stormed into the room.

"Is Luke here?" I demanded. Just this week she had asked about him, wondering who the boy was who had been picking me up for school. I had no intention of letting them meet. I was furious that Luke took that decision away from me.

Mom nodded. "I told him he could wait for you in your room."

"You sent him to my bedroom?" I twisted around and marched up the narrow staircase. Of course she sent him to my room. Otherwise she would've had to enter the real world long enough to entertain him until I got home.

I took a breath in front of my partially closed door. I steeled myself before opening it, trying to shake away any sign of how emotional I felt.

He was seated in my desk chair, his large body out of place in my small room. He swiveled my way when he heard me enter. He held a pen in one hand and he continued to *tap-tap-tap* it against my desk even as I stood there glaring at him.

"Your mom let me in." His blue eyes were crinkled at the corners, his forehead creased with concern.

"So I heard." My arms were crossed tightly over my chest. My movements felt jerky and unnatural. I didn't feel comfortable in my own space as I edged closer to Luke. I wanted to pluck the pictures from the edges of the frame on my mirror. I wanted to stuff them away somewhere private, somewhere that would keep my secrets safe.

I knew it was already too late. I could tell by the look on his face. Pity. Confusion. His expression was full of questions.

"Want to tell me what this is?" He motioned to the pictures. Pictures of Sydney and me. In the oldest of the pictures, my red hair was in pigtails. I was holding a squirming baby. In another, I was giving my toddler sister a piggyback ride at the beach. In the last one, Sydney was in a hospital bed, smiling though looking weak.

He looked away from me. His eyes rested on the picture in the frame. I had her drawings scattered all over my room. But that one? It was the most important to me.

It was a colored pencil drawing. Three figures stood on the sand, the rolling waves of the ocean crested behind them. Carefully scripted over each of us were our names: Mommy, Daddy, Megyn. Floating in the air above us all was our angel, in the way she envisioned herself toward the end. Her heart healthy and strong, encased in a pair of wings.

"Want to tell me what you're doing here?" I countered.

He hung his head and had the decency to look sheepish. "I was being selfish. And stubborn. I figured you really didn't have plans today. I stopped by to ask you one last time if you would come to Leo's with me."

"Didn't his party start, like, an hour ago?"

"Yeah."

"How long have you *been* here?" I was equally as furious with my mother as I was with him. Thinking of him alone in my bedroom all this time left a squirmy feeling in my stomach.

"Awhile."

"Then you can go." I managed to untangle my arms from where they were looped over my chest. I jabbed my finger toward the door. "Now."

He stayed put. "I don't think so. Not until you talk to me."

I recognized the stubborn set of his jaw. He was a guy who was used to getting what he wanted. I didn't have the energy to deal with him. I was emotionally drained. I wanted to be left alone.

"Luke." My tone was a low warning. "I don't want you here."

"I know."

"Then please leave." My voice cracked and tears blurred my eyes. I blinked hard and pinched the bridge of my nose. I didn't want to cry in front of him. My frustration was getting the better of me. It made me feel weak, and I hated feeling weak.

"Meg," he said quietly, finally rising from the chair. He had to duck, mindful of his head and my low ceiling as he moved to the center of my room. He walked toward me slowly, as if I was an injured kitten he thought might bolt. "I didn't mean to upset you. I want to talk to you."

"I don't have anything to say."

He cupped his hands around my elbows. "That's not true. I think you have a whole lot to say. I want to listen." He paused, as if he thought his monologue would rattle my words free. He pressed ahead. "The girl in the pictures, she's your sister?"

I didn't want to answer him but how could I not? Not answering felt like I was denying the truth. I could never deny Sydney, or what she meant to me.

I nodded.

"And…" He cleared his throat, seeming to choose his words carefully, but we both knew there was no good way to say what he needed to say. "She died?"

Again, all I could do was nod.

"Oh, Meg, I'm so sorry. I had no idea. Why didn't you tell me?" He gave my elbows a squeeze, gently tugging me forward.

I resisted and took a step back but that didn't put enough distance between us. I pulled free from his grip and turned away from him.

"I didn't tell you because it's none of your business."

"Sure it is." His tone was quiet and insistent. "We're friends, right?"

I closed my eyes and pulled in a few deep breaths, hoping maybe I could seal away the renegade tears that seemed intent on escaping.

"Meg?"

"Yes." My voice was high-pitched, scratchy. "We're friends."

"Then talk to me. What happened to her?"

It wasn't that I didn't want to tell him. I felt like I couldn't. My throat was so constricted it felt as if a giant fist was holding it in its grip.

"Can you at least tell me how long she's been gone?"

"A year," I said, my tone finally flat and not chaotic. "She's been gone a year today."

I flinched when his hand settled on my shoulder. He twisted me around but that didn't mean I had to look at him. I kept my gaze averted, stuck to the calendar on the far side of my room. He tucked me into a hug that felt more comforting than a summer's worth of sunshine.

"I'm sorry." His words were simple, but I felt the sincerity behind them. "I'm sorry I pressed you so hard about today."

"You didn't know."

"Because you never told me." He glanced at the pictures again. "What was her name? How old was she?"

"Sydney. She was twelve."

"What happened? Was it cancer…or…?" He left the question dangling because he didn't have another guess.

"It was her heart." The words choked me as I forced them out. "She was diagnosed with a rare form of pediatric cardiomyopathy when she was ten. She was such a little fighter. We were lucky we had her in our lives as long as we did." I gnawed on my bottom lip for a moment, hoping Luke would say something. When he didn't fill the silence, I did. "The disease is most often fatal. She was on the list for a heart transplant. She had already had multiple corrective surgeries. There's no cure, but it bought her some time." I shrugged, giving myself a few more seconds to put my words together. "A heart never came and time ran out."

He glanced at the picture in the frame again. The heart encased by a pair of wings. I could see the realization dawning on him, taking hold.

My sister's creation was my signature piece, my way of remembering her and honoring her. An angel, taken too young, finally set free.

"I had no idea you had a sister."

"You would have no way of knowing. She was at the middle school until she got too sick to attend. Then my parents pulled her out. Mom stayed home to take care of her."

"If I'd known what the murals represented, I never would've pressured you into this deal." He scraped his hand through his hair. "I feel like such a jackass."

"I haven't minded all that much." I realized I meant it.

He looked embarrassed and very much like he didn't believe me. "No wonder you never wanted me to come around. Your life is complicated enough right now. I thought you were…"

"Being difficult?"

"I'm sorry I showed up here today. I was acting like an entitled ass. I'm sure I'm the last thing you or your mom wanted to deal with."

I couldn't really argue that point so I let it slide.

"Luke," my voice was firm, "you should go to Leo's."

"I don't want to leave you."

I dropped down on the edge of my bed. "I want you to go. I'm not really in the mood for company. Truly, I'm not."

"Right. You need to be with your family. I'm sorry I

intruded." His body language was screaming that he didn't want to leave me. But more than anything, I needed him to go. "Are you sure there isn't anything I can do for you?"

"Please." It was all I could manage to say.

For once, he listened. He leaned in and kissed my cheek. Then he left me without another word.

Chapter Seventeen

I was totally zoned out, pretending to listen to Trevor and Colton tell a story about some wild party they went to. I did not want to be here. I did not want to be listening to this bullshit.

I'd felt like a creeper, hanging out in Meg's room without her there. I'd been pissed when Jaclyn had been in mine. I knew it had to be even worse for Meg. But once I walked in, I couldn't leave. I knew there was a story there—especially when I saw the drawing with the angel's wings—but I'd needed to hear the words from Meg.

A hand squeezed my elbow, long fingernails gently digging in.

I turned around with a scowl, expecting Jaclyn.

"Hey," Julia said. "Can I borrow you for a minute?"

"Yeah," I glanced at Adam who gave us a quizzical look. I didn't care. I wanted to get out of there. "What's up?"

"Just come on."

I followed her as she zigzagged through the crowd. She probably needed help moving a table or something. We walked toward the front of the house. When we turned the corner, the last thing I expected to see was Meg pacing in front of the garage.

"Someone wanted to talk to you," Julia said.

Meg twisted around at the sound of her voice. Julia gave her one of those finger-wiggle waves, squeezed my shoulder, and left.

"I was hoping you'd look happier to see me."

I closed the distance between us slowly. After I left her house earlier, I wasn't sure she was ever going to want to talk to me again. I wrapped my arms around her, squeezing her into a hug. Her arms went around my waist, and she held on tight.

I pressed a kiss to her temple before I let her go.

"I'm happy," I assured her. "I'm just surprised."

"I thought I wanted to be alone. But I really don't. Is it okay that I'm here? I promise I won't be a downer." She motioned down the street. "Kylie gave me a ride. The weather looked questionable. I'm supposed to text her if I'm staying."

"Yes, stay." That would explain why I didn't hear her drive up. My ears had become weirdly attuned to the Rebel. It always grabbed my attention, even when I wasn't expecting it.

She sent her text and slid her phone into her pocket.

"Are you okay?"

She winced. "I'd be better if you didn't treat me like something was wrong."

"Done. I do have one question."

She grimaced. "Luke, I really don't want to talk about Sydney."

"It's not about Sydney."

"Then what?"

"Megyn?" I lifted my eyebrows. "I had no idea your name

was Megyn."

Apparently there was a helluva lot about Meg I didn't know.

"Oh."

"I like Meg. It suits you better."

"Thanks. I think."

"It was a compliment. 'Meg' sounds like a no-nonsense kind of name."

"And I'm a no-nonsense kind of girl."

"Exactly. It's one of the things I like best about you."

She wrapped her arms around her waist and glanced around. No one was on this side of the house but a lot of noise was coming from the backyard.

"Why didn't you just come and find me?"

"I was going to, but I saw Julia first. I wasn't sure if you still wanted me here. I didn't want to cause a scene so…"

"Got it. Ready to go face everyone?"

She nodded. I slung my arm around her shoulder.

"You didn't tell anyone, did you?" she asked. "There's a reason I keep it to myself. I hate the way people look at me when they find out."

"I haven't said a word. That's your secret to tell."

We rounded the corner and bounced to a halt when we found ourselves face to face with Jaclyn.

"And what secret would that be?" Jaclyn demanded.

"The secret way she manages to drive me crazy." I tugged Meg a little closer. She did not need to deal with this today of all days.

Her lip curled. "Yeah. I can imagine. Is that why you're slumming it?"

"I'd watch your mouth if I were you, Jac."

"You're the one who needs to watch it, Luke. Your parents aren't real happy with you right now."

"And how happy would George be if he knew why we

really broke up?" I asked. "The bigger question is what would your extremely devout Catholic mother think?"

"You are such an ass," she hissed.

"I'm the ass? I let you walk all over me." I jabbed a finger her way. "Stay the hell away from me. Stay the hell away from my girl. Maybe then I won't fill your parents in on what kind of person you really are. The best thing you ever did for me was cheat on me. It was the wake-up call I needed."

I sidestepped her, pulling Meg along with me.

I bypassed the tent that was set up as a precaution against rain. I needed a minute to pull myself together and thought maybe Meg could use one, too.

We took a seat on a bench in the garden.

"I'm sorry," I said. "I know this is a rough day for you. I shouldn't have gotten into it with her. I should've walked away."

"You *really* liked her." Meg studied me with a look that was quizzical but not judgmental.

"*That's* what you got out of the argument?"

"I heard it in your voice when you were arguing with your mom at the restaurant, too."

"We were together a little over a year. I've known her since we were kids. Funny how I didn't really know her at all. She played me. She was playing me the entire time."

"Why would you say that?"

"I know you don't pay a lot of attention to my friends, but she and Julia used to be BFFs, or whatever. She'd been messing around on me for a long time. Maybe even the whole time." I'd never actually confessed this to anyone. "Julia finally told me about it. She'd known for awhile. I think because she was with Adam, she was having a hard time keeping it to herself. Knowing her friend was cheating on her boyfriend's best friend? And keeping it from him? Anyhow. She eventually came to me. I didn't believe her. She told me where I could find Jaclyn. And. Yeah. I found her all right."

"I'm really sorry."

She slipped her fingers around mine.

It made me feel like crap. She shouldn't be trying to make me feel better, not today.

"Like I said, at least now I know." I forced my tone to be light. "When I caught her, she freaked out. She begged me to take her back. For awhile I even considered it. I was such an idiot. You know what's even more messed up?"

"What?"

"Julia told me the reason Jaclyn was chasing me so hard. Her *dad* wants us together. How twisted is that? He got it into his head that Dad's going to make him partner. Dad's current partner, Frank Holbrook, is retiring soon. Mr. Winters wants to buy out his share of the firm, but there's already an agreement that Dad is buying him out. By next year the firm will be Prescott and Prescott." Unless Gabe truly defected, but that was Dad's problem to figure out. "With our families' history, I guess he thought if Jaclyn and I were together, he'd have a better shot."

"She still wants you back?"

"A few months ago she was laying it on thick. Saying she missed me, promising she wouldn't mess up again. Putting her off was exhausting. And then that night, I was out for a run, trying to clear my head and get some perspective on the situation…"

"You caught me—"

"I was feeling so desperate," I finished. "I wanted Jaclyn off my back. I knew the only way to do that was to make her think there wasn't a chance. My head wasn't in the right place to date someone for real."

"Hey. Prescott. Get your ass over here," Adam bellowed. "We're going to have a team meeting."

I motioned to Adam to let him know I heard.

"I better get over there." I stood and waited for her to follow, disappointed that we were being dragged away.

• • •

I stared up at the dark window, mentally berating myself because I was about to do something stupid. And totally lame.

I hit Meg's number on my speed dial. Maybe she shut her phone off at night. Or silenced it. Or maybe not, I realized when she answered on the third ring.

"Luke?" She sounded groggy. Not a surprise.

"Hey, Nutmeg."

"Do you know how late it is? Why are you calling?" Her voice was soft and sleepy. She sounded content all curled up in her bed.

"I know exactly how late it is. I'm calling because throwing a rock at your window seems like kind of a cliché."

Her next words were sharp, as if she'd snapped herself awake. "My window?"

"Also, it sounds questionable. With an arm like mine," I joked, "I was afraid I'd bust the glass."

Three seconds later her curtain was shoved aside.

I waved.

She waved back.

"Come outside?" I urged.

The curtain fell, and she disconnected. I stood there looking up. Had she hung up on me because she thought I was crazy? Maybe I was crazy.

The front door swung open and she slipped through it. She was wearing yoga pants and a black hoodie. Her hair was twisted into a sloppy, sexy mess on top of her head. A few strands fluttered around her face.

"Hi."

"Hi," she replied.

The sound of a vehicle cruising down a side street melded with the sounds of crickets chirping in the distance. We stared at each other a moment, neither of us seeming to know what to say.

"Why are you here?" she finally asked.

"I wanted to see you."

"You spent all evening with me."

"I know. Didn't seem like long enough. I ended up stuck in a team meeting. You had to hang out with Julia. I feel like I didn't really get to see you at all."

Amusement lit up her eyes. "Are we just going to stand here on my sidewalk?"

"Wanna go for a drive?"

She nodded, and we hurried down the block to where I parked.

I had no idea where I was going as we skirted the edge of town.

"Slow down. Slow down." Meg slapped her hand against the dashboard.

"What? Why?"

"Please."

I did better than slow down. I pulled over to the side of the road.

She leaned forward, craning her neck so she could look skyward. Laurel's water tower was probably a hundred feet in the air. It was stark white and stood out against the starlit sky.

"Are you checking out the water tower? It's not new. It's been here, like, forever," I said.

"I know. I've never *noticed* it before." Her eyes were sparkling. Excited energy radiated from her.

"No."

"What?" she shot back.

"Meg, you can't really be considering painting the tower." I tried to sound reasonable. "How much painting have you done since the high school?"

"None," she said, all wide-eyed innocence. "I've been good. *Really* good. But this would be perfect. It's ideal."

"It's *illegal*."

"There is that," she cautiously agreed.

"We're talking not only vandalism, but trespassing. It's fenced in. There's barbed wire topping the fence." That should be a deterrent, shouldn't it?

This was *not* what I had in mind when I asked if she wanted to go for a drive.

"I don't plan on climbing over. There's a gate. That little piece of linked chain just needs to be cut and the door will open right up. It's nothing that a little old bolt cutter can't contend with."

How could she sound so reasonable when she was so obviously edging on insane?

"It's not happening." That was an order.

She said nothing.

"It's not only illegal. It's *dangerous*." I suddenly felt as if I were the rational guy trying to talk a jumper off a ledge. Only I wasn't doing a very good job, judging by her twitchy excitement level.

She leaned back against the seat and made a vague motion with her hand. "You're right. It's a dumb idea. Let's get out of here."

I studied her, noting the way her hands were clenched tightly in her lap. Her feet had the smallest bit of bounce to them. Her bottom lip was clamped firmly between her teeth.

"You're a terrible liar," I accused. "You're going to paint the tower the first chance you get."

"You should come with me," she said excitedly. "The ladder starts…what…eight feet up? We come up with a makeshift ladder that reaches the real one. It's easy-peasy. It's like this tower is asking to be climbed."

"If anyone is asking for anything, it's you." I shook my head. "What you're asking for is your very own arrest record."

"Okay," she shrugged. "Don't come. It's better that way."

"You're *really* going to do this? What if you fall to your death?" Had that thought crossed her mind? "No one would find your body until morning."

"I won't fall." She sounded so sure. "People climb water towers all the time."

"You know this?"

"I'm guessing."

"Well it's a horrible idea."

She grabbed my hand. The excitement in her tone had faded to a desperate plea. "I need this."

Something in me shifted.

"Why the tower? There's got to be a nice brick building in town. Another overpass? A parking lot?"

"I want that." She pointed out the windshield. "It's the first thing people see when they come into town. It's the closest I can get to the sky."

To Heaven. That's what she really meant.

"I'm basically going up a ladder. What's more natural than climbing a ladder?" She sounded so reasonable. "That's what they're made for."

I rarely admitted defeat but realized I was not going to win this argument. Meg's stubbornness would not be taken out by my common sense. The anniversary of her sister's death was probably the worst possible day to have to talk her out of this.

"When are you doing this?"

"I have no idea. It's not like I've formed a plan yet."

I pulled back onto the road. "Promise me one thing."

"Maybe." The girl knew better than to promise at random.

"Let me know before you go through with it."

"That," she said, "I can do."

Chapter Eighteen

MEG

Two days later I crept out of the house minutes before midnight. The moon was full. It was the best sort of night for painting. Dark enough to blend in, but light enough to see what was right in front of me.

I sprinted down my steps, down the sidewalk, and continued on down the block.

Luke was waiting at the corner.

The dome light lit up the cab for a moment. I didn't bother to suppress my smile when I realized he was dressed in all black.

"Criminal is a good look on you."

"Oh, yeah?" he asked, half laughing. "We all know you have the ninja look mastered."

"I might have to pull out some ninja moves if I'm going to climb that tower."

He tossed a plastic bag in my lap.

"What's this?" I pulled the bag open before he had a

chance to answer. I found a black hat and a pair of gloves inside.

"The gloves are the sort you use for rock climbing."

I ran my fingers over the palm, noting how they would help with my grip.

"And I thought a ski mask would be smart, just in case," he said grimly.

I tentatively held up what I had thought was a hat. It was, indeed, a ski mask.

"I figured if I'm going to be your partner in crime, I might as well dress the part."

"Actually," I said quickly, "it was impulsive of me to ask you. I don't want you to get in trouble. You could stay on the ground. Be my lookout?"

"I can't stand the thought of you climbing that ladder alone. Which," he said, "I know is stupid. It's not like I'll be able to catch you if you fall. But still."

We drove in silence. My palms were sweaty. I was grateful to Luke for his foresight and purchase of the gloves.

"Are you nervous?" He pulled up to the curb a few blocks away from the tower.

"Kind of. I've never been nervous before, but then again, I've never had someone else's reputation at stake," I admitted. "I've only ever had to worry about myself if I got caught."

"Let's be sure not to get caught then."

We hopped out of the vehicle. Our synchronized footsteps echoed softly as we hurried down the deserted sidewalk. My cans of paint clanged familiarly in my backpack. Most of the houses lining the street were dark. The field where the water tower stood was directly before us.

I felt a moment of trepidation as my gaze went up, up, up to the sky. The moon shone down, lighting the field in an eerie fashion. Now that we were so close, I noted the tower was taller than I had realized. My nervousness faded as adrenaline kicked in. I was doing this for Sydney, and that gave me the courage I needed. I picked up my pace. Luke adjusted his stride to keep up.

We reached the fence that enclosed the base. Four sturdy metal legs led to the top. A cage-like ladder was attached to one of the legs. It was tubular, with rungs circling all the way around to keep a person from falling backward. The ladder started a good eight feet up.

I rummaged around in my backpack, pulling out what I needed.

"Let's do this!" I tugged on my ski mask and gloves. I pulled out the bolt cutter. I put it in place and gave the handles a squeeze. It took more effort than I anticipated. Luke reached for it, a silent offer to do it for me. I shrugged him away. I wanted the breaking and entering to be on my shoulders.

With a *crack* the deadbolt snapped. I hurriedly unwound the chain. I tossed it to the ground and shoved the gate open.

I put the bolt cutter away and pulled out a carefully rolled up bundle.

Luke took one final look around as he pulled the gate shut.

"Coming?" I asked.

"Yeah." He laced his fingers together. I held the bundle I had pulled from my backpack in both hands. I stepped into Luke's makeshift hoist, just as we'd discussed. He catapulted me upward.

Being a worrier, Mom had purchased a rope ladder for my second floor bedroom. It was the sort of ladder that hooked onto a windowsill and reached the ground in case of a fire.

The moment he lifted me high enough to reach the rungs of the water tower ladder I hooked the emergency ladder to it.

I quickly found my balance with the foot that was not in

Luke's hand. Once one foot was on the ladder, I stepped on with the other foot.

In no time I realized how helpful the gloves were. My hands easily gripped each wrung. As a trickle of perspiration dribbled down my spine, I knew my hands would've been sweaty and slippery. The climb would've quickly become treacherous.

There's a fine line between fear and rapture. When your adrenaline kicks in, even the direst of circumstances can create a euphoric rush. I scaled the hundred or so feet, not with ease, necessarily, but not with difficulty, either. I was a misbegotten superhero on a mission.

When I emerged at the top, my muscles were trembling from the exertion. I clambered onto the narrow walkway that encircled the tank. A waist high guardrail offered some security. I dropped my backpack onto the metal grated floor as Luke appeared.

He looked over the edge and then quickly pressed himself against the tank. "I don't think I like heights very much," he admitted.

"You're just realizing that now?" I pulled my black spray paint from my bag and uncapped it while keeping an eye on Luke. "Are you going to be okay?"

"Sure. Yeah. I haven't exactly been in this kind of situation before. I'll be fine." He stayed seated while I got to work. Both of us were puffing and panting. Our breathing eventually evened out as our bodies relaxed.

Once I began, reality faded away. It was almost as if I could feel Sydney watching over my shoulder. I could hear the echo of her laughter and envision the way her eyes would light up. Maybe I should've felt sad, but I didn't. For the time it took me to complete the mural, I felt *free*.

Luke let me work in silence, correctly guessing I would work faster without any interruptions. As I painted he didn't budge from his spot. A quick glance at him every now and again confirmed he was scanning the street below, watching for any sign of trouble.

I finally finished and took a step back. I bumped into the guardrail. Luke jumped to his feet.

"Don't get so close to that." He swayed and grabbed the railing. "Yeah. Not a fan of heights." He twisted around to get a look at my work. "It looks…good. I bet it would look even better from the ground."

I laughed but he was right. I knelt down and repacked my bag.

"We should get moving," I agreed.

He scrambled to the edge and began the descent. I shoved my hands back into my gloves and quickly followed.

We had barely begun when a dog started to bark. At first I thought it was coming from the neighborhood across the street. It was Luke who realized it wasn't.

"Uh, Meg?"

I quickly zeroed in on what he had noticed.

Wagging its tail and yipping his welcome was an enormous, shaggy beast of a dog.

"Damn it."

"Right," he agreed. "Keep moving."

"Dexter. Here, boy." The voice echoed through the dark. Even as I continued to move downward, my head swiveled around. I scanned the neighborhood. I didn't see anyone, but that didn't mean anything. The voice sounded far away. I could only guess it would edge closer.

"Move, move. But don't fall. I'd rather end up caught than dead," he called out to me.

He was right. Getting caught would suck. But I *really* didn't want to end up in a casket or with my bones shattered into a billion pieces.

I had worried the euphoria would fade once my painting

was done. I had worried exhaustion would set in, making going down a struggle. Instead, with this looming threat, a new wave of adrenaline coursed through me.

We moved downward in quick, methodical movements. Each footstep carefully placed. We were moving as much by feel as by sight. The moon shone brightly, and while it gave us the advantage of better night vision, it would also give anyone walking by a better view of us. Not that anyone would even be looking if it weren't for the damn dog.

The nearer we got to the ground, the louder and more excited Dexter became. I could see him running back and forth, pacing, tail slashing through the air.

"Dex—" The owner stopped mid-yell. I twisted my head to the left and saw the silhouette of a man standing on the opposite side of the street. "Hey," he called. "What are you doing?"

The back of my shirt was soggy. I was sweating like a cow and cussing like a sailor. The ski mask felt itchy and damp as it became plastered to my face.

"Hey, you!" the owner bellowed. "You can't be up there. I'm calling the cops."

"Thanks for the warning," Luke grumbled.

"Stay where you are," he called. "Dexter will rip you to shreds if you come down."

I was sure the only danger we were in from Dexter was being slobbered on. I was thankful that Luke had, for no real reason, swung the gate shut on our way up. The dog couldn't get too close to us. Not yet.

I could tell the man was on his cell phone. I couldn't make out his words. It didn't take a valedictorian to infer that he had called the cops.

The solid metal ladder ended, and my feet hit the less stable rung of the rope safety ladder. A siren split the air. It wasn't close, but it wasn't as far away as I would like.

"Worried about the dog?" Luke asked.

I glanced over my shoulder. Dexter danced around happily. Tail wagging, tongue lolling about. *Now* his barking ceased. "Nah."

"Don't move!" the man shouted.

"Guy's probably planning on making a citizen's arrest," Luke scoffed. I felt his hands around my waist as he pulled me from the ladder and dropped me to the ground.

"Let's get out of here," I encouraged. "I'll take my chances with the mutt."

A flurry of fur lunged at Luke when he pulled the gate open. He swung his leg out in a sweeping motion. It didn't hit Dexter but the dog yelped anyway. It was surprised, but not deterred. A moment later his big paws landed on Luke's chest. He stumbled as the dog's slobbery tongue slashed out for a lick. Cussing, he pushed the dog away.

We took off running, and Dexter, despite his owner's bewildered hollering, was on our heels. I yanked my bottle of pepper spray from my pocket as we raced across the field.

"Sorry, boy." I slowed my pace for a moment, aimed, and fired a small puff. Dexter let out an awful series of yips that made me feel like a monster. It did, however, stop him in his tracks.

The owner let out a cry of terrified indignation. "What did you do to my dog?"

I faltered but Luke grabbed my hand. "The dog will be fine."

This was no time to argue. The silent night had turned into a cacophonous onslaught. The man was screaming obscenities at us, Dexter was yowling in pain, and the siren was shrieking as it grew ever closer.

Luke pulled at my hand, leading us to the backside of the field, away from his vehicle.

"Aren't we going the wrong way?" I huffed.

"We're going to take the long way around." We hit the tree line, and he let go of me. We raced through the woods as quickly as we dared, and I let him take the lead. We stumbled a few times, tripping over fallen logs, tangles of weeds and other debris. I dared a glance over my shoulder. The siren had been silenced. Now blue and white flares cut menacingly through the darkness.

We came through the other side of the trees, spilling into a neighborhood. My muscles were screaming and pain shot through my side. My lungs ached but we didn't stop running.

I wasn't sure where he was headed, but I continued to follow.

"This way," he instructed over his shoulder.

He cut across a yard and I jogged after him. He darted toward an enormous wooden swing set. Three swings lined one side, a tower with a slide stood on the other. We clambered up the ladder on the backside.

We both dropped to the wooden slatted floor. We were both gasping for air, our lungs burning, our chests heaving.

"Figured," he said through gasps, "this was...an okay... place to hide."

The rough wood felt heavenly beneath my worn-out body. A metal roof covered us, but the wooden sides only went halfway to the roof. Big wedges of sky were visible in between. Blackness was ripening into a deep plum. The sun would be rising soon.

"We left the ladder," I said.

"I know."

"Can they use it as evidence?" I wondered.

I felt him shrug beside me. "They can try. But I don't think it'll be very useful. It's not like you can take fingerprints off rope. Unless they trace the sale?"

"No," I said. "Mom bought it from a secondhand store years ago."

"Good. Then it can't be traced." He hesitated and then growled, "Damn, we got lucky."

"I know."

The seriousness of the situation slammed into me. We had *almost* been caught. What if Dexter hadn't been a friendly dog? What if one of us had slipped on the way down? What if the cops had gotten there a few minutes sooner?

This could've ended so differently.

He brushed his knuckles against my cheek. "Are you okay?"

Was I?

"I don't know." I rolled my head to the side to look him in the eye. "This time felt different."

"Painting the tower will be pretty hard to top."

I let his words sink in, and I realized something. "It would be impossible. It wouldn't make sense to even try."

"So that's it? You're done?"

"I'm done."

His hand reached for mine. "Then I'm glad I was able to be a part of it."

I squeezed his fingers. "So am I."

Chapter Nineteen

MEG

"I hurt everywhere," Luke announced. "It's your fault."

I hadn't expected him to answer the door in nothing but a pair of swim trunks and a lopsided grimace. He gripped two towels under his arm. His biceps bulged around the bundle. I'd learned that he was able to throw a consistent eighty-mile-an-hour fastball with that arm.

"I know." I hobbled inside. I tried to concentrate on the ache in my thighs in an effort to distract myself from his obnoxiously chiseled abs.

School had started a few hours ago. When I first got up, I told Mom I wasn't feeling well. It wasn't exactly a lie. She excused me for the day, and I went back to bed. Luke woke me up with a phone call and an offer to use his hot tub.

My muscles begged me to comply.

I let Mom think I was heading to class. I knew she wouldn't call. She'd just assume I'd check myself in.

Luke and I had stayed in the wooden swing set until we

were sure we hadn't been followed. Eventually we'd climbed down and trudged back to the SUV in silence. We'd stuck to the shadows as we looped away from the water tower, adding several extra blocks to our hike, but feeling safer because of it.

By the time he'd dropped me off, molten streaks of sunlight were cresting the horizon.

"I have aches in places I didn't even know existed," he grumped as I followed him down the stairs. "And that's really saying something because the coach at the last baseball camp I went to was a sadist."

"Imagine how I feel. You are definitely in better shape than me."

"It's the offseason," he argued. "I *hurt*."

"Poor baby."

He led the way through the game room, out a set of double glass doors and onto the patio in the backyard.

The water bubbled invitingly.

He tossed the towels onto a lounge chair before climbing the steps to the hot tub. I quickly wiggled out of my clothes, glad I'd thought to come dressed in my bikini. The hot water felt heavenly as I slid in.

I rested my head against the hard-rimmed edge. "I feel better already."

We were quiet for a while, relaxing, allowing our aching muscles to be massaged by the jets.

Eventually he asked, "Nutmeg?"

His cautious tone made me suspicious. "Yes, Luke?" I mimicked.

"I know about Sydney. I know your mural is a copy of her work. But why do you do it?" He squinted at me over the bubbling water. "I get it to some extent. But I feel like I'm missing something."

I had to organize my thoughts, trying to find a logical way to answer that.

"Sydney wanted to be an artist. She was young, so maybe it was a phase. But she said so many times she wanted to see her artwork all over the world. Obviously that's never going to happen. One night, about a month after she died, it hit me. I could do this one piece, this one thing to honor her memory. Honestly? I was such a mess, I didn't think about the consequences at first."

He didn't say anything, so I kept talking.

"The first two I did were on buildings I knew were going to be torn down. I guess you could say they were my trial run. I wasn't sure if I'd be able to pull off a decent mural. But the design was pretty simple."

"How many murals are there?" he pressed.

"There's an old barn on a busy road north of town. It's crumbling, beyond repair. The property is abandoned. I also painted an old wooden fence. It's up on a hill so anyone driving by will see it. Half of the fence was missing and the rest was in pretty bad shape." I continued on, listing landmarks I'd hit. "Some of them are as far as twenty miles away. For the most part I've chosen surfaces I didn't think mattered to someone else. Structures that are highly visible, but unsalvageable."

"The overpass?" he asked.

"Someone had already tagged the opposite side. I guess at the time I felt justified."

I braced myself for the question I knew he was going to throw my way.

"Why the school, Nutmeg? It's almost like you wanted to get caught."

"Maybe I did."

I'd suffered through dinners with Luke's family. I knew how imperfect his parents were. Because of that it wasn't hard to tell him the truth.

"The school is the one place I did on impulse." I rolled my lower lip through my teeth, trying to figure out how to explain this. "My parents haven't been the same since Syd died. They either fight or ignore each other completely. The night I painted the mural they had a horrible fight. Mom couldn't stop crying. Dad locked himself away in his room."

I felt tears burning in my eyes and my throat was tight.

"I knew I was being reckless but part of me didn't care. In the back of my mind I thought so what if I got caught? Maybe then my parents could focus their anger on *me*, instead of each other." A sarcastic laugh bubbled up. "The irony? The moment I crashed into you I *knew* I never wanted them to find out. I knew it would make things worse. It was stupid and impulsive and when you caught me, it was the *worst* kind of reality check. I've regretted that decision every day."

"Guess you're lucky it was me."

I nodded because yeah, I really was.

"The water tower?"

I dropped my gaze. "That's different. It was worth the risk." The water tower was more visible than all of the other places put together. People could see it for miles.

"That's about Sydney."

"Yes. It's in a place everyone can see. They might not know what they're looking at, but *I* know." I shook my head. "I'm sure this all sounds so stupid to you."

"I'm not judging. Not when I've done things I regret, too."

I assumed one of the things he regretted was helping me with the tower.

"What would your parents do if they found out about last night?" I asked. "Bail you out? Pull some strings? Cover the whole thing up?"

"Probably." I had been joking, but he sounded serious when he answered. He also sounded disgusted. "Dad wouldn't allow me to tarnish the family name. Ironic considering the sleazy way he makes a living."

"Is it really that bad?"

"I think it is. Most of his clients are guilty. These corporations have enough money to pay a top lawyer to help them weasel their way out of trouble." He made a sound of disgust. "I realize it's the nature of the business, but that's not the kind of life I want to live. I'd rather struggle to pay my bills than be rolling in blood money."

"Have you told your dad this? That you don't want to work for him?"

"I talked to my mom. She's the more reasonable one. She said Dad would probably cut me off. I asked her how good of a lawyer I could possibly be if I hated my job. She said Gabe isn't crazy about his job, and he does just fine."

"Basically she was telling you to suck it up and deal with it."

"Pretty much. They don't know this yet, but Gabe's had enough. I think he's going to walk away soon. He said he'd rather be a construction worker than spend another year at the firm."

"If you don't want to be a lawyer, what do you want to do?"

"I want to go into sports medicine. A few years ago I sprained my ankle. It ended up not being a big deal, but I was really worried at first that I wouldn't be able to play. I saw a physical therapist, and he really helped me."

"That's something your dad wouldn't approve of," I guessed.

"No."

"What's wrong with going into the medical field?"

"He sees it as a personal insult that I don't want to follow in his footsteps. He rattles on and on about how hard he's worked. How he's paved the way for his sons. He thinks we should be grateful because if we follow his plan, our futures will be set."

"You're not supposed to live your own life?"

"Not if he can help it."

"You should talk to Miss Perez."

"The guidance counselor?" he asked skeptically.

"She's pretty awesome. Tell her you want to explore college options without involving your parents. She'll help you. She has a knack for looking at things from a different perspective."

It appeared as if he was actually thinking it over.

"I'll figure it out," he finally said. "That's enough serious talk for now. How do you feel about going to another party?"

"What kind of party?" I narrowed my eyes at him. "If it's a party that involves your parents, I'd rather decline."

He laughed lightly. "No. No parents."

"What is it then?"

"Adam's dad owns a big chunk of land north of town. It's kind of in the middle of nowhere. It's beautiful, really. A river runs through it, and a few times a year we camp out there."

"Camp?"

"Camp. With tents." He rushed to add, "Well, Adam has a camper set up, so there are some amenities. But the rest of us rough it."

I mulled the idea over. I didn't hate it. But I didn't love it, either.

"Who will be there?" I asked.

"Me…hopefully you. Adam and Julia. Leo and maybe a couple of other guys. Trevor usually comes but I'm not sure what he'll do."

I wrinkled my nose at the thought of Trevor. Wherever he was these days, Jaclyn tended to follow.

"When you mentioned tents, you meant sleeping in them. Overnight?"

He held up his hands and shot me an innocent look. "Just two friends, sharing a tent."

"Right." Could it really be that simple?

He nudged my foot. "Hey, don't read too much into this. I don't have an ulterior motive. I'm offering because I know how much you like to get away. You'll have a good time. I promise. It's pretty laid back. We have a bonfire. Adam never invites a lot of people. That way it stays pretty mellow."

An entire night in the woods. With Luke. In a tent alone? It was probably a horrible idea.

"Okay, I'll go."

"Really?"

The way he smiled at me lit up my insides, confirming this was definitely a very, very bad idea.

"Yeah, why not?" After the nerve-wracking ordeal last night, it sounded like a great way to relieve some stress.

"I think last night was a bonding moment," he teased.

"You do realize," I said cockily, "that you can't blackmail me anymore."

He nudged my foot again. "Why is that?"

I gave him a triumphant grin. "Because as of last night, you are officially my accomplice. You can't turn me in without getting yourself in trouble."

"I never intended to turn you in." He flashed an innocent smile.

"Really?" I wasn't sure I believed him. "You definitely fooled me. You seemed awfully determined to get your way."

His lips twitched. "I *was* determined to get my way. That's why I had to play hardball. I had to make you believe I wouldn't hesitate to go to Mr. Prichard."

"You were very convincing," I admitted.

"I'm glad you're still playing by the rules. It's honorable of you," Luke said. "One rule, in particular."

"Which rule would that be?" I cocked my head to the side, as if I didn't know.

"The 'Luke can kiss Meg whenever he wants' rule."

I gave him a serious nod. "That's my favorite one."

He reached over and wrapped his hands around my waist. My body bobbed through the water as he effortlessly positioned me on his lap. My knees rested on either side of him. Our chests pressed together, and his lips were so, so tantalizingly close to mine. His hands skimmed up and down my bare sides, heating my skin a million degrees more than the water of the hot tub ever could.

When he pulled me in for a kiss, I was sure I was about to combust.

Chapter Twenty

Luke

"I have to admit I'm surprised you agreed to this," I said.

"I'd rather be just about anywhere but home these days." She tried to keep her tone light, but I knew her parents' relationship was weighing on her. "Every time I think the tension can't get any worse, it does. You could've asked me to go shopping with your mother and I probably would've agreed." She wrinkled her nose. "Or not. I'm not that desperate. Yet."

Meg had become so willing to spend time with me, I'd let my ego get carried away. For a while there, I thought maybe she was falling for me. Comments like that reminded me that I was little more than a distraction for her.

A distraction. I didn't like that. At all.

"What's wrong?" Meg bumped her shoulder into mine.

"Nothing," I said. "Maybe we should get back to the group."

"It's so peaceful here." It was getting dark. The other guys were busy with the fire, but Meg asked to see the river that ran through the property. It wasn't far from the campsite. She sighed as she turned away from me. The water looked like ink as it flowed past us. The scent of moss hung in the air. In the distance I could hear our friends laughing.

The campsite was already set up. We guys had grilled burgers, and Adam's mom had packed a crazy amount of food.

Meg had told her parents she was staying at Francesca's.

"Luke," Adam bellowed, his voice carrying through the woods. "A little help here?"

"Yeah," I shouted back. "That guy does not grasp the concept of kindling. If I don't help him, he'll probably douse the logs with gasoline, light a match and call it good."

"You better help him then. Wouldn't want the entire campsite to go up in flames."

"Exactly."

Meg followed me back to the clearing. She ducked into the camper to check on Julia while I neared the fire pit as Adam tossed in a match. Heat whooshed through the air as flames shot skyward. They quickly receded, wrapping around the now glowing stack of logs.

I spotted a can of gasoline tucked up against the camper. I shook my head.

"What?" Adam said. "I got it going, didn't I?"

"I thought you wanted my help." Wasn't that what the yelling had been about?

"You were off with Meg," Leo said. "He didn't think you'd come back."

Adam grinned at me as he pried the lid off the cooler. He took out three beers, one for each of us. I held on to mine, feeling like I needed to check with Meg first. I could take it or leave it. Our coach was strict. He didn't hesitate to bench players who broke the rules. Out here, no one would know

I was breaking the rules. Still, I didn't want to make Meg uncomfortable.

"Don't want it?" Adam motioned toward the bottle in my hand.

"I want to make sure Meg doesn't care."

"Julia really likes her," Adam said. "She was glad you invited her."

"I wish she would've brought Kylie," Leo mumbled.

I smacked him on the shoulder. "I mentioned it like I said I would, but Meg didn't bite. Maybe if she knew why I was asking…?"

Leo shook his head.

"Maybe next time," I offered.

Only a few of us had shown up tonight. No wonder Leo looked so glum. Guy was so shy. No way did he have the guts to invite a girl.

I took a seat on my green blanket. Meg had spread it out before our walk in the woods. I clenched the cold bottle in my hand.

"Hey you." Meg tapped my foot with hers. She held an enormous mug, similar to the one Julia held.

"Hey." I held up my bottle. "Mind if I drink this?"

"Go for it." She dropped down on the blanket next to me. She inhaled the scent of her drink and hummed her appreciation. "This is the best cocoa I've ever had. The fire feels good, too."

It did feel good. The temp had dropped significantly now that the sun had set.

Half an hour later I was well aware of something that felt even better. My back rested against a tree. But Meg? She rested against me. She'd settled herself between my legs. One hand gripped her cup, the other my knee. Or my thigh. Or any part in between. With her body pressed against mine it was impossible to get away from the scent of her perfume, from the heat of her. When she laughed, her body vibrated against my chest.

My thoughts backtracked to the other day. Us. In the hot tub. My hands wandering. Her hands wandering. Kisses so intense I was sure my mind was blown. I needed to get my thoughts away from Meg because I was enjoying myself a little too much.

I redirected my attention to the conversation that I'd been missing.

"Trevor isn't here because there's a party at Colton's. His last few parties have gotten completely out of control," Julia explained to Meg. "The cops showed up and everyone ran. I'm not sure how his parents still let him get away with having parties."

"His dad is golf buddies with my dad," I grumbled. "He's managed to bully Colton's way out of trouble."

"Remember his last party?" Adam asked. "Bethany and Meredith thought the hot tub would be prettier if it was pink. They dumped an entire punch bowl into the water."

"Idiots," Leo muttered.

"I'd so much rather hang out with just a few people," Julia said.

"This is really fun," Meg agreed.

Julia tugged herself away from Adam. "I'm going in for a refill," she told Meg. "Do you want one too?"

"Sure." Meg, usually pretty graceful, stumbled a bit as she got to her feet. I kept my hands around her waist to steady her.

"Looking a little tipsy," Adam said with a grin.

"*Ha.* Hardly. It's only cocoa. But it was soooo good." She giggled but stopped when she noticed Julia's eyebrows shoot up.

"Um, no, actually it isn't." Julia's face scrunched in apology.

Meg held her oversize mug up and studied it a moment, as if it could tell her what was going on.

"It's hot cocoa and butterscotch schnapps?" Julia's words rose at the end, questioning how this could've been missed. "Heavy on the schnapps. Just the way I like it."

"Ohhhh," Meg dragged out the word. "That's why it tasted so good! I thought it was, you know, really expensive cocoa. Like, from Belgium or something."

"I thought you knew. I guess I mixed that one before you came into the camper. Are you sure you want more?" Julia asked.

Meg nodded. "Definitely."

"Don't get my girl drunk," I warned. Everyone laughed, including Meg. I wasn't joking. Was alcohol the reason her hand had been coasting up and down, driving me half insane?

"We'll just keep her a little tipsy." Julia winked at Meg to let her know she was joking. The two of them disappeared inside the camper.

She was back minutes later, settling in against me again, as if she belonged there. It kinda felt like she did.

"I thought you didn't drink?" I whispered the words next to her ear.

She turned to face me, her lips grazing my cheek. "I don't. I didn't. I mean, I haven't ever before."

"You're a bad influence, Luke," Adam jibed.

Julia swatted him playfully. "It wasn't Luke's fault. It was mine."

• • •

When the fire finally died down, we all went our separate ways to bed. Without the flames to heat the air, the night had become frigid.

Meg's teeth chattered and banged together as she

burrowed down in her sleeping bag. She had changed into a pair of leggings and a sweatshirt. Before I'd turned off the lantern she had zipped her sleeping bag to the top so only her head was sticking out.

"You okay over there?" The tent was decent-size. I'd placed Meg's sleeping bag as far from mine as I could. It was a lousy attempt to help me resist temptation. I was tempted as hell. I just wasn't going to act on it.

"It's f-freezing. I'm used to a room with a heater. And w-walls."

It was colder than the original forecast had predicted. Meg sounded miserable; I felt guilty. I should've grabbed an extra sleeping bag. I waited a few minutes, hoping she would warm up so the chattering would stop.

When it didn't, I grabbed her sleeping bag and tugged her toward me. I could feel her shivering through the thick fabric.

She groaned. "I think I drank too much. The tent is spinning."

I laughed. "The tent isn't spinning. I'm just moving you."

I quickly unzipped our individual sleeping bags so I could zip them back together, making one big sleeping bag. Without dislodging Meg from her cocoon, I slid in next to her.

"Come here," I ordered. "You'll warm up faster."

She wiggled herself over to me. I had planned on scooping an arm around her to try to keep her warm, but she had her own plan. She tangled her body around me, resting her head on my shoulder.

I was frozen, afraid to move. The friction of her body against mine was enough to knock my common sense into the next county. She shifted and her hand drifted into my hair. Her lips skimmed against mine. I wrapped my arms around her, cursing myself for getting drawn into her kisses. When her hand slid down my body, the sensation slammed some sense back into my head. I *wanted* her to keep going but I *needed* her to stop.

"Meg?" I gently pushed her away.

"What?" She was more breathless than I was.

"You should get some sleep. You had a couple of drinks tonight."

"So?" Her body slumped against mine.

"So we should slow things down." I tangled my fingers around hers, mostly to get them into safer territory. "You've never had alcohol before."

She sighed as she curled her body into mine. "It's not the alcohol."

I pressed a kiss to her forehead. "I just want to be sure."

We might have agreed to no strings, but there were definitely lines. I wasn't going to take advantage of the situation and cross them…no matter how much I wanted to.

Chapter Twenty-One

"Luke."

"Shit! Jaclyn!" I bounced backward on the sidewalk. "Where the hell did you come from?"

She wedged herself between me and the door of Common Grounds. I took another step back. I narrowed my eyes at her. "Did you *follow* me?"

"You told my mom about Drew?"

"Drew? Who the hell is Drew?" Realization dawned. "Ah. One of the guys you cheated on me with. Found out there were so many, I can't keep track of them all." An exaggeration, but still well deserved.

"So you did."

"Actually I didn't. I have no idea what you're talking about."

She grated out, "My mother knows."

"Jaclyn," I said, struggling for calm, "you can't sleep with half the town and expect that word won't get around."

She drew back to slap me but my reflexes were superior to hers. I held both of her wrists in place. Maybe accusing her of sleeping with half the town was a bit much but I wasn't going to apologize. When she took a step back, I released her.

"Why can't you just leave me alone?" I asked. "We're not a couple. We're never going to be a couple. We will never even be friends. Why can't you just back off?"

"I was backing off," she said coldly. "Until you stirred things up."

"How did *I* stir things up?" I was at a loss.

"Are you listening to anything I say?"

"Is this about Drew?" I guessed.

"Yes, you idiot."

"If she knows, she didn't hear it from me. I don't exactly go out of my way to talk to your mom. If you haven't noticed, I work pretty hard at avoiding your whole damn family."

"Really? Because she knew about Dad's office."

My stomach dropped. That had to have come from my mom. Okay, no wonder Jaclyn was so pissed. I'm sure her extracurricular use of Prescott office space didn't sit too well with her mom *or* mine. At the same time, I felt a weird sense of relief that Mom had actually believed me.

"You know what my mother is like." She glared at me with more hatred than I'd felt from her before. Considering how the last few months had gone, that was saying a lot.

"Don't blame me for your mistakes."

"I'm blaming you for not keeping your mouth shut."

"Me?" I scoffed. "You started it by turning it around on me. You told your mom, knowing she'd tell mine, that I'm the one who cheated. Do you know how insulting that is? I had to set the record straight. I had that right."

She opened her mouth, ready to go another round. This could go on indefinitely, I knew from past experience.

I sidestepped her and reached for the door. "Forget it. I'm

not doing this with you. If your mom is pissed, then maybe that's exactly what you deserve. You need to stop acting like a spoiled, entitled princess. Take responsibility for your own actions for a change. This is *not* my fault, so let it go."

She slammed her hand against the frame, keeping it closed.

"Let it go?" She shook her head. "I don't think so. Thanks to you, my mom practically has me on lockdown."

"She can't have you locked down too tightly. I mean…" I motioned to her, standing right there in front of me. Blocking my way again.

"I just came from church! She thinks she can stop me from seeing Trevor. I have an asinine curfew. I'm required to be home for dinner *every* night. Did I mention the lectures? The *neverending* lectures? I'll let it go when you're as miserable as I am." She gave my shoulder a pat. "That's a promise."

Her words settled like a stone in the pit of my stomach. The feud between us had been going on for months now. My gut instinct was telling me there was no way it was going to end well.

It was hard to remember a time when we'd actually gotten along. When things started going downhill, they really took a nosedive.

I pulled the door open. I kept walking. I'd never let her know how much she rattled me.

I spotted Meg tucked away in a back booth. Her head was down as she doodled on a napkin. Her hair fell forward, like a curtain, blocking out the commotion of the morning crowd.

I stopped a few feet away.

Watching Meg instantly calmed the chaos crashing around in my head. I stood there for a minute, just taking her in. I didn't see her as the same girl who had sashayed into Maebelle's. She had been all hard edges and feistiness. The Meg I'd gotten to know was funny, vulnerable, and a perfect mix of sweet-sass.

As I stood there, I realized something.

The little criminal had a hold of my heart.

Suddenly I was itching to get out of there. I wanted to take her somewhere so I could have her all to myself. For weeks we'd been living in a gray area. My threat of blackmail had slipped into a no-strings relationship. It was probably time we hashed this out and determined what was really going on between us.

Falling for her was *not* part of the original plan. But as she turned to me and smiled, I realized it had been a stupid plan anyway. Maybe it was time we reassessed this no strings thing.

"Hey, you."

"Sorry I'm late. I got caught up."

I was already late before my run in with Jaclyn. So late that Meg had a half dozen napkin doodles going on.

I dropped down across from her. "Maybe you should just get a tattoo. Then you can have it with you all the time."

"Maybe someday I will." She pushed the napkins aside. "Are you okay?"

If she hadn't noticed the drama on the sidewalk, I wasn't about to drag her into it. I glanced around. I didn't see Jaclyn. She must not have followed me in.

"I'm fine." I strummed my fingers on the table. "I think we should get something to go. The weather's decent for a change and there's somewhere I want to take you."

She leaned forward, her eyes widening with interest. "Where?"

"You'll see when we get there."

I hopped up and she scrambled after me.

"That's not fair. Give me a hint."

"No," I laughed. "There's no point in giving you a hint. Now what do you want? Let's get in line."

• • •

"Well," Meg said as she glanced around, "this is kind of remote."

We stood in a weed-infested parking lot. The pavement was cracked, missing chunks in places. We were on the backside of a brick building with boarded windows. It stood in the center of what was now an overgrown field.

Cars periodically whizzed by on the road out front. I chose this place because I could park in back and no one could see us.

"It's an old factory. It went bankrupt in the nineties. Now it's just sitting here because it's full of asbestos. Clean up would cost more than what the land is worth."

Her arms were crossed over her chest. Her eyebrows were scrunched as she nodded. "Fascinating. That does not explain why we're here."

"I thought maybe you'd want to mess around." I started toward my SUV.

"I don't know, Luke." She skipped along beside me, tapping the bill of my ball cap, making it sit cockeyed. "This place doesn't exactly scream romance. It kind of screams bodies buried in the basement."

I gave her a look. "That's not what I meant. I meant mess around with these." I reached into the open window of my backseat and pulled out a box.

She gave me a quizzical look before taking it. "Sidewalk chalk?"

"I know you said you were done with the graffiti. I also know you miss it. I get that this isn't really the same. No one will see it back here, but I also saw your face the night you sprayed the tower." She enjoyed the process. I had no doubt about that. "You were totally lost in your work. I could tell you were thinking of your sister, and it made you happy."

I don't think she realized it, but she doodled on everything. Napkins, scraps of paper, the sand, black marker over her black boots. The notebook with our rules was full of her quick sketches. I'd been driving around with the chalk for awhile, waiting for some free time and some decent weather. When I spotted the stack of napkins, I thought why not offer her a building? I was familiar with this one. Dad had been part of a few of the asbestos related lawsuits the company faced.

"Is it lame? It is." I winced.

She set the chalk on the hood and pulled me in for a kiss. Her fingers dipped into my back pockets. She tugged me closer. I returned the favor, wrapping my arms around her, pressing her body into mine as the kiss deepened.

Oh, yeah. My heart had definitely been hijacked.

"I love this." She eyed up the building when she moved away. "It's like a magical canvas. When it rains, the chalk will wash away. Poof. Gone. I can start all over again."

I gave her a nudge. "Hop to it."

"Oh, no. I'm not doing this alone." She grabbed my hand and towed me along.

"What am I supposed to do?" I asked. "I was kinda looking forward to sitting back so I could watch you in action again."

"I'll take this side," she moved to the left. "You take that side."

A door split the two sides down the middle.

She set the chalk in front of the door, selecting the red chunk before moving to her side of the building.

"Nutmeg," I grumped. "What am I supposed to draw? I'm not artistic."

She was not sympathetic. "Pick up the chalk and draw from your heart."

"Sure thing." I grabbed a piece of chalk and stood back. I watched as she got busy.

She caught me admiring. With a stern look she pointed at my blank wall. "Get to work, mister."

I moved forward, feeling like a kid, and began to scribble.

Eventually Meg sidled up next to me. She patted the top of my head. "I knew you could do it."

"Ha," I said. "Ha ha."

Her eyes sparkled. I loved to see her happy. She picked up the box of chalk, and we moved back to my Navigator. From this vantage point we could see both drawings.

Hers was detailed, the contouring of the angel wings making them look multi-dimensional.

Mine? It looked like a toddler drew it. But I have to say, I got the appeal. Sketching something out like that? It was relaxing. Now I understood why half the teachers at school had those adult coloring books.

"It looks good," I told her.

"So does yours. The baseball bat? Very realistic. And the ball is in perfect proportion." Her tone was mock-serious as she continued to critique. "I'd give it at least a six. Maybe a six plus. You should've thrown in a glove, might've jacked you up to a perfect ten."

Her phone chimed in her back pocket saving me from trying to defend myself.

She dug it out. "It's Francesca."

"Aren't you going to answer?"

"I'll call her later."

"Good. Because there's something I think we should talk about."

She propped a hip against my driver's door and waited.

I shoved my hands in my pockets. "So. I was thinking maybe we could…maybe we should…"

I faltered. I hadn't really thought through what I was going to say. Meg had said she didn't want anything serious. She *did* have a lot going on in her life. That hadn't changed. In some ways, it seemed to be getting worse. Her parents were constantly on her mind. I didn't want to push her. I readjusted my cap and kicked a piece of chipped asphalt. It skittered across the lot.

"This conversation is extraordinarily exciting," she teased.

Her phone rang again. She frowned. "She usually texts. Maybe it's important."

She wandered away to take the call. When she twisted around and headed my way again, I knew instantly something was wrong. Her face was white. Her expression anxious. She disconnected and let the phone dangle from her hand.

"Nutmeg?"

"Francesca just saw a copy of this morning's paper. The water tower is on the front page. They're offering a reward in addition to the one offered through the school."

Front page of the Sunday paper?

Yeah. We were screwed.

Chapter Twenty-Two

MEG

The following week Francesca didn't freeze me out completely, but I definitely felt an unprecedented chill factor emanating from her. She had warned me; I hadn't listened. I was constantly catching Kylie watching me with what looked like pity.

She thought I was going to get caught.

I probably deserved to.

I had spent days trying to come up with a way to make things right.

I took a risk and righted one of my wrongs the only way I knew how.

Dad's store sold paint. We also had access to industrial strength paint remover. Donning work gloves, goggles, and a safety mask, I had crept back onto school property at night, undoing the damage I had done.

Unlike the blissful calm I had felt all the nights I'd painted the murals, last night as I stripped the wall bare, my heart pounded painfully hard. It felt a little bit like I was scrubbing away the memory of my sister.

With the help of his coach, Luke had spent the week creating a video of his game highlights. He was trying to make connections with college coaches. He and Adam decided some off-season conditioning wouldn't hurt. They'd either gone to the batting cages or the weight room every night after school.

I think he knew I was in a petulant mood and needed some space.

By the time the weekend rolled around, we'd hardly seen each other.

I was feeling better today. The school was scrubbed clean. No one had come forward, despite the reward in the paper. I'd managed to come up with an idea that felt like a retribution of sorts.

As I pressed Luke's doorbell, I told myself I was there because I wanted to share my plan with him. My heart told me that wasn't the only reason.

I missed him.

He frowned when he opened the door. "Meg. What's going on? Is something wrong?"

I understood his concern. I'd never just shown up at his house before.

"Not really," I said. "There's something I want to talk to you about."

"Come on in." We traipsed up the stairs. He was obviously doing homework. He was wearing a pair of LHS sweats and a well-worn baseball jersey. His hair was rumpled and his feet were bare.

I followed him to his sofa and sat down next to him. In front of us, notebooks, pens, and textbooks were strewn about.

"You look busy."

"Yeah. Dad's on my case about my grades again. At first I was pissed, but then I realized that might not be such a bad thing." I arched an eyebrow in question. "My grades are good. I've made the honor roll every semester. You got me thinking… A while ago you mentioned other options for college. It never occurred to me before, but I might be eligible for something other than a baseball scholarship. Maybe an academic scholarship? Or maybe both?"

"You really want out from under your family, don't you?"

"Yes, but you already know that." He shifted so he was sitting sideways facing me. "You've kind of been a stranger this week. What's up?"

"I've been thinking. I realized I needed to undo some of the damage I've done." I told him what I'd done to correct my mistake at the school.

He winced. "It would've been ironic if you got caught *cleaning* graffiti."

"I know. It was nerve-wracking. I'll get to the overpass eventually. The water tower…" I winced. "That's another story. I thought about climbing it again, whiting the whole thing out."

"That would be stupid," he said. "You'd be caught for sure. I'm betting police are still patrolling the area."

"Right."

"You're not going to turn yourself in." It was a command, not a question.

"I probably should…but I'm not." No matter how wrong I'd been, I was a coward. I couldn't bear the thought of paying the full consequence for my actions. I hoped my own personal penance would be enough.

"This week I joined the Ecology Club at school. They clean the city parks, pick up garbage out of ditches, whatever needs doing. I know it won't undo the damage, but at least I feel like I'm trying. I know it's not the same, but I hope it counts for something."

"Maybe I should join with you," he offered.

"You've got enough going on. You were already really busy this week with Adam." I motioned to his stack of homework. "If your dad is on your case about grades, I think the Ecology Club can get along without you."

He didn't look terribly disappointed by my refusal. I couldn't blame him. It wasn't going to be nearly as much fun as tossing around a baseball.

"Oh." A wayward thought crept into my head. "I have something for you."

"*You* have something for *me*?" He leaned forward like a little kid and waited.

I rummaged around in my messenger bag. I pulled out a book.

"I know it's not much. I saw you flipping through my copy of *The Outsiders* the other day." It was the latest required reading for my American Lit class. "I thought maybe you wanted to read it. I bought you your own copy."

"Thanks." He gave me a sheepish grin. "It's been on my reading list for a while. I can't wait to cross it off."

"You have an actual list?"

The tips of his ears turned pink. "Did I say that out loud?"

"You did." I laughed. "Want to hear something funny? Kylie's in AP English. She said *The Handmaid's Tale* isn't on the reading list this year."

"Um…" His face scrunched.

I patted his knee. "It's okay. I find it absolutely adorable."

"Adorable? I don't think anyone has called me that since kindergarten." His hand slid across the cushion. His fingers tangled around mine.

The threat of blackmail had fizzled the day we were in the hot tub, probably way before then. I wasn't sure what was going on with us anymore. The rules of our relationship had blurred a long time ago. I had thought I didn't want anything serious. But spending time apart this past week had made me realize something.

"I missed you," I blurted.

His other hand slid up to my cheek. "I missed you, too."

He leaned in and pressed a kiss to my lips. I backed away before it got too intense.

"Remember when we used the sidewalk chalk?"

"Nutmeg, it was last weekend."

"Right. But do you remember what you wanted to talk to me about? Before Francesca called?" I had been sure he wanted to talk about *us*.

A sharp, quick succession of knocks erupted from the other side of Luke's door. Without waiting for a response from him, his mother swung the door open.

"Meg," she said, "we're having company this evening. I'm hosting a dinner party for several lawyers at the firm. I would appreciate if you would move your...*motorcycle* out of the driveway."

She said the word as if it tasted bitter in her mouth. It was not a subtle hint. She wanted me to leave.

"The caterers will be arriving shortly. I don't want you blocking their way."

Luke didn't let go of my hand as we crossed his room.

"I'll see her out," Lenore told him.

"Mom—"

"It's fine," I assured him.

"I'll call you when the dinner is over so we can meet up." He gave my hand a squeeze. "I think we really need to finish this conversation."

"Conversation?" Lenore's tone held an arctic chill. "Is this something your father and I should be aware of?"

"Nope," Luke said, keeping his tone light.

Lenore motioned for me to get moving. She guided me down the hallway, down the stairs, through the foyer and out the front door without a single word. I didn't care. Unless I was reading Luke all wrong, she'd be seeing a lot more of me whether she liked it or not.

· · ·

" — not going to continue like this." Dad shouted.

I winced and edged down the staircase. I'd been listening to music, trying to get ahead on homework while I waited for Luke to call. There had been a long lull between songs, and the fight had pierced the gap.

"What were you thinking?"

"I don't know," Mom shouted back.

Mom. Shouted.

It was an incongruous thought, like finding a parakeet on the kitchen table. The two didn't mesh. Mom didn't shout. Mom barely ever engaged. A chill ran through me because I realized this must be serious. I waffled in the hallway, wondering if I should interfere or hide out in my room. My curiosity pinned me in place. I felt trapped, curiously wanting to listen, but guilt telling me I should give them privacy.

"This has to stop *now*," Dad bellowed.

"What do you want from me?" Mom asked tiredly.

"I need you to see a therapist. You need to get straightened out. If you won't do it for me or Meg, do it for yourself. You're in a downward spiral. You. Need. Help," Dad's tone was firm.

I edged into the living room. "What's going on?"

Dad looked startled to see me but quickly recovered. "Your mother has been taking sleeping pills."

"So?" That was nothing new.

"Not *just* the ones prescribed by her doctor. She's managed to get additional prescriptions by going to doctors out of town." He cast her a disappointed look over his shoulder. "She has an entire stash of them. She even has a few bottles of over-the-counter ones. She's damn lucky she hasn't overdosed."

"Mom?" She shifted her attention to me. "Why would you do that?"

"I…" Her voice was barely above a whisper, "I didn't want to *feel* anymore. They relaxed me."

"They turned you into a zombie." I thought it was depression that caused her to sleep her days away, to spend a worrisome amount of time in bed. But she'd been drugging herself. Even when she was awake she always seemed so out of it. "Dad's right. Do you know how easily you could've overdosed?" A frantic thought took hold. "Is that what you want? To be with Sydney again? Are you so desperate to see her again that you're willing to leave us?"

"No, sweetie." Mom squeezed past Dad and moved toward me. "That's not it at all. Don't ever think that."

"What am I supposed to think?"

"You're supposed to know that I love you," Mom said, the patience I remembered from my childhood glimmering through.

"Then prove it. Get help. See someone. Talk to Miss Perez," I begged.

"Marion," Dad said, "what would a little bit of counseling hurt? Won't you at least try?"

"I don't see the point," Mom argued. "It won't bring Sydney back. It won't change anything."

I took another step back. "You can say you love me, but actions speak louder than words. You have done *nothing* to prove it since Sydney died. I miss you. You're right here, and I *miss* you." My voice cracked, and my dammed-up tears finally broke with it. "Sydney didn't choose to leave us, but you," I pointed an accusatory finger at her, "you *choose* every single day, you choose to distance yourself from your family. I get that you're hurting and you don't want to be. But none of us want things to be the way they are. Everything we do in life is a choice. If you won't try to get better for yourself, I wish you would choose to get better for *me*. I need you. Both of you."

I yanked the door open but paused for a moment as I cast a glance over my shoulder. "Sydney would *hate* this. Seeing what has happened to the two of you, to our family, it would break her heart."

Mom put her hands over her face, and her entire body shuddered. Dad slouched in defeat.

I had nothing left to say. I grabbed my coat, slammed the door, and barreled out into the night. A light mist was coming down. Not enough to drench me, not enough to sway me from leaving.

I yanked my helmet out of the sidesaddle and pulled it over my head as I tossed my leg over my bike. For just a moment I sat there gripping the handlebars to tame the trembling in my fingers. I pulled in a deep breath, willing my tears away. I was so sure my parents would come after me. When they didn't, my heart cracked just a little bit more. I stuck the key in the ignition and the Rebel roared to life. I looked back at my family's house one last time as I pulled out of the driveway.

Chapter Twenty-Three

LUKE

My bedroom door swung open without warning. I glanced up from *The Outsiders* to see Dad filling my doorframe. He gripped a snifter of brandy. His posture implied an impending attack. I tossed the book aside and got to my feet.

"Luke," he started, "your mother is pretty unhappy right now."

"How is that my problem?"

"She knows you spent the night with Meg up at Adam's place last weekend."

"How would she know that?"

"I understand how rocky things are between you and Jaclyn. But she still cares about you."

Jaclyn? I'd ignited her wrath and now my ex had launched a sneak attack.

"We don't think Meg is a good fit for you. She wouldn't be the first woman to use her wiles to snare a man." He sipped his brandy. "Your mother doesn't want you meeting up with

Meg tonight, or any other night."

My stomach twisted.

"Now I don't care if you mess around. We all need to sow our wild oats from time to time. I know how easy it is to get caught up in the moment. You forget about protecting yourself. She tells you she's on the pill. You hit the sheets. Next thing you know, you're hit with a paternity suit. Some women see nothing but dollar signs."

"She's not like that." I knew this was an argument I would never win.

"I've done some digging. The girl spent a few years in therapy. There's no telling how messed up she still is. Your mother is beside herself worried that you're tangled up with some head case."

I wondered if he knew about Sydney. If he did, it was clear he didn't care.

"Fooling around with a girl like Meg is one thing. I see the appeal. But you need to end it before you're tied to that girl for life. You've got a bright, successful future ahead of you. It does not include getting ensnared by some girl."

"Meg's not just some girl. She means a lot to me. I know you don't respect that, so I don't see the point in discussing her with you." I dropped back down on my sofa and swiped up my book. It was the best way to show I had no interest in what he had to say. He yanked the book out of my hand.

"Dammit, Luke. Her family is drowning in debt. How do we know they aren't behind this? Maybe they encouraged their daughter to attach herself to a rich young man."

"Or maybe she just happens to like me."

He surprised me by saying, "Maybe she does." He grunted as he settled into the chair across from me. He pulled out his reasonable tone, the one he used when trying to convince a jury to see things his way. "We both know your mom isn't going to let this go. How about you make it easy on me? There're a lot of pretty girls at your school. At your age girlfriends come and go. Don't ruin your future for a fling. You're young. Have some fun. Move on to the next one."

"I'm not ending anything."

My father studied me. "Of course you are. I just need to know what it's going to take. Everyone has a price, Luke. What's yours?"

His question didn't shock me, in fact, I'd been expecting it. He was so predictable. In his world, there was nothing money couldn't fix.

"I don't have a price."

Ignoring me he said, "What will it be? An upgrade on your SUV? An all expense paid ski trip for you and the guys? I could make another sizable donation to that nonprofit you were so interested in last summer."

"You're bribing me with charity?" I shook my head in disgust.

"How about that camp in Colorado? You still want to go? Get rid of Meg and consider it done." When I didn't say anything, he got up and walked out without another word.

My blood sizzled through my veins. I was angry at his offer and even angrier at myself for knowing he would make it. This was playing out just how I'd wanted it to. Just how I'd planned the day I'd blackmailed Meg into being my girlfriend.

Only now, I regretted it all.

• • •

The possibility of a full-ride was finally within my grasp. The only way to hold onto it was to push Meg away. Funny thing was, the camp didn't seem so important to me anymore.

Meg felt like the only stable thing in my life. No way was I giving her up. I'd done some research. I could find some other way to get through college. If Meg could do it, so could I.

Dad could take his offer and stick it.

I tossed a selection of ties on my bed, trying to decide which one would annoy Mom the most. Any minute now she'd be hounding me to greet our guests.

A crinkling sound caught my attention. I twisted around. Someone shoved a lavender envelope under my door. Probably Mom's sarcastic way of inviting me to come down for dinner.

It felt weirdly spongy. I dumped out the contents on my desk.

It was a stack of napkins from Common Grounds.

A half dozen napkins covered in Meg's doodles. Not *just* doodles. But doodles that looked a hell of a lot like the mural on the school.

The sight of them was so surprising it took a minute to wrap my head around it. Realization started snaking around in my brain. This could be bad.

Beyond bad.

Who...?

My phone pinged, the alert for a picture. Jaclyn's name popped up. Dread started pumping through my veins.

It was a shot of the mural on the high school.

I dropped onto my desk chair.

Another ping.

The water tower.

Another ping.

Another photo.

My heart slammed and my palms began spewing sweat. Jaclyn had warned me outside of Common Grounds that she was going to make my life hell. She had everything she needed by the end of the day. She was sitting somewhere, loving this.

My fingers were gripped so tightly around my phone, I wouldn't have been surprised if it shattered. Jaclyn had followed us from Common Grounds. I'd thought the building was private. No one from the road could see us—but we couldn't see them, either. Jaclyn obviously found the napkins, followed us, parked nearby, and then crept through the woods. She was probably hoping to nail us for trespassing or...who the hell knew what she'd been hoping for.

What she'd gotten was a whole lot more.

A photo of Meg standing in front of her nearly completed mural at the factory glared back at me. It was a shot of her in profile only. But all that red hair would give her away.

Another alert sounded. I jabbed at my screen.

Jaclyn: *Guess whose daddy owns a paint store? Meet me in your gazebo.*

She was ruining me from my own backyard.

Thunder rumbled, rattling my windows. Rain hadn't hit yet but a storm was definitely brewing.

I shoved the napkins in my desk drawer and my phone in my pocket and rushed down the stairs. I could hear the chatter of a few guests. Mom would be looking for me any minute. I flung open the back door and darted across the lawn.

Jaclyn was right where she said she'd be. The air felt electric with the storm coming in. Lighting flashed in the distance, flickering across Jaclyn's face, distorting her features. She looked like the evil witch she was.

I stomped into the gazebo.

"You have no idea how hard it's been to sit on this for a week." Her voice oozed confidence. "It was worth it, just to be able to do it in person."

"You can't—"

"Don't make excuses. If I take this to the police, it's all the evidence they would need to launch an investigation. It's the same artwork, Luke. The pictures speak for themselves."

She was right. If the police questioned Meg, she wouldn't deny it.

"I thought you wanted to hurt me. Why are you going

after Meg?"

"Figure it out. You two have been like Velcro. I figured the best way to get to you is to use her."

"You're going to turn her in."

"That is one option." She smiled. "Would you like to hear option two?"

Did I have a choice? "You obviously want something. What is it?"

"I know you. You're needy. You have this obsession with needing people to like you."

"It's called being a decent person. You should try it."

"Maybe some other day."

"What do you *want*?"

"I want you to end things with Meg."

"What? Why? You don't think you and I still—"

"Don't be so conceited. Dad will never make partner so why waste my time on you?"

My heart hammered. Why was she doing this now? Now, when Meg and I were finally moving toward *really* being together.

"Look at it this way, if I go to the police, I get to take down Meg. But this way, I get to take you both down. Two birds, one stone. Right?"

"So I'm just supposed to break things off?" I tried to hold an even tone. I didn't want her to know how much this mattered to me.

"I'm going to need a little more than that." Her tone was playful. She was loving this. "I want to know she'll never take you back."

"No." I felt sick. I felt worse than sick. I felt like I was being shredded apart from the inside out.

She held up her phone. "Break her heart, or I'll ruin her future."

I had to find a way out of this.

"You've been treating me like I'm dirt. It might've taken me a while to figure it out, but the whole time you were dating a girl who's wanted by the police. You had to know. You were at the abandoned building drawing with her. What right do you have to be so critical of me?"

"You're right." Maybe she *was* right. Maybe I'd been too hard on her. "I'm sorry. Can we talk about this? Can we think it over?"

"I've been thinking about it all week." Her tone was matter-of-fact. "I told you what I want. I'm not going to sit through another dinner having you toss condescending looks my way. I'm tired of your arrogance. But I'm willing to make a deal with you."

"Jac—"

"You have daddy issues. You don't want to be like your father. You're such a...*people–pleaser*. You're so nice to everyone. But you've been *really* awful to me." She stuffed the phone back in her pocket. "I think you need to be taken down a few notches. Make her hate you."

I raked my hand through my hair. "How am I supposed to make her hate me? What am I supposed to say?"

"Tell her you've been with someone else. That's why you hate me, isn't it?"

It was only one of many reasons.

She shrugged. "I'm sure you'll think of something."

Rumbling floated through the air. For just a moment I thought it was thunder rolling in. Horror snared me when I realized it was a motorcycle. More specifically, Meg's Rebel. I could pick out the frequency anywhere. I flicked my gaze toward the road.

Jaclyn laughed. "Oh, Luke. This couldn't have worked out more perfectly."

The engine quieted as Meg parked on the street.

This couldn't be happening.

"No time like the present," Jaclyn gloated. "You might as well get it over with. If you don't, I'll make sure the dinner conversation is *captivating*. Imagine what a table full of lawyers, employed by your father, will think about you dating a bona fide criminal."

My phone rang.

Jaclyn's smile lit up her face. "Answer it."

I turned away from her. "Hey, Meg."

"Can we talk? I know you have the dinner party. It's probably a bad time."

It is the worst possible time.

Jaclyn looped her arm through mine, then squeezed in warning.

I cleared my throat. "No. It's okay. I'm actually in the backyard." Big, fat drops of rain burst out of the sky, plopping against the ground. "We can talk in the gazebo."

When I spotted Meg, her arms were wrapped tightly around her waist. Even in her riding gear, I knew she had to be cold. The yard light lit up her face. Her hair whipped around in the wind. Her lips were trembling.

"Meg?"

"I needed to see you." Her voice sounded off-kilter. "I was hoping we could talk."

She kept a few feet between us as a bolt of lightning split the sky. The roar of thunder rolled closer. Dizzying flickers followed. Jaclyn watched from the back patio. There was no way she could hear us, but body language would tell her everything.

I began to pace. My mind was spinning. Words started pouring from my mouth faster than I could think them through.

"Yeah. I've been meaning to talk to you for a while. The deal we made? There's more to it than I let on." I had her attention. "I needed leverage."

"Leverage?"

"The night I caught you vandalizing the school, it got me

thinking. I hoped pretending to date you would be enough to push Jaclyn away, but the real reason I needed you to pretend to date me had to do with my parents."

"Because you wanted your mom to back off."

I shook my head.

"Then what…?"

"I knew they wouldn't want me to date you. The motorcycle alone was enough to tip my mom over the edge. Not to mention my dad. He's all about appearances. I knew they'd want me to end things. And they did. Right away, they did." I was rambling. I couldn't stop. "But we continued on with this…this arrangement. The longer we pretended to date, the more frustrated they've become. Now I have them right where I want them."

"What does that mean?" Her voice shook.

"If I don't see you again, they'll sign the papers for Colorado."

The weight of my words seemed to crush her. She looked like she was folding in on herself.

"You needed me to be your pretend girlfriend because you knew I would be an *embarrassment* to your family?" Her voice was cold. "You wanted them to disapprove of me. You wanted them to hate me. That's why you let them rip me apart the night of the ball. You never once stepped in to defend me. You wanted them to think I was nothing but trash."

"I've never thought you were trash." How could she think that?

"You *used* me."

"You knew this relationship wasn't supposed to be real." My heart was beating so fast I thought it might explode. This was so much worse than I thought it would be. I thought she'd be *pissed*. I didn't think she'd be *crushed*.

"What I *knew*," she shoved my chest, "was that you needed some space from Jaclyn. You never said *anything* about the rest of it. You handpicked me for what…my *freak* factor?"

"*No*," I choked on the word. "You're different. That's a *good* thing."

"Is it?" Her voice cracked. "It worked in your favor that I only wear black, that I drive a motorcycle, and that I live in the crappy part of town."

I was going to find a way to destroy Jaclyn if this didn't kill me first.

"The worst thing? You *made* me fall for you. You tried so hard to win me over. What was the point? You're worse than your father. He's awful, but at least he doesn't try to hide it."

I wanted to grab Meg and run. I wanted to beg her to let me explain things better. I wanted to do it without Jaclyn lingering in the shadows.

Meg swiped at her face, wiping away tears. "I came here tonight because this has been one of the worst nights of my life. And that was *before* this insane conversation. I thought seeing you would make me feel better. You've made me feel a thousand times worse."

She bolted into the downpour before I could stop her.

Every cell in my body was screaming at me to go after her. I couldn't let her leave. Not like this. I ran out into the rain, digging in my pocket for my keys. I raced around to the front of the house where my vehicle was parked. The Rebel roared to life in the distance.

I had to weave my way out of the driveway, past all the guests. Rain smeared my vision, even with my wipers on. My headlights cut into the darkness. I stepped on the gas, trying to catch up with Meg before she got away.

Her taillights glowed red in the distance. I was gaining on her. I breathed a sigh of relief. Then a car whipped around the curve ahead, swerved into Meg's lane, and my world imploded.

Chapter Twenty-Four

MEG

My mind was fuzzy. My eyelids felt thick, sticky. My body ached and nausea rolled through me. When I finally managed to pry my eyes open, the bright light sent a slicing pain through my skull. I slammed my lids shut again.

"Meg? Sweetheart?" Mom's voice was soothing even though it crackled with concern. "I'm right here."

My eyes fluttered open. Mom's face was a silhouette against the fluorescent light behind her.

"It's okay. Don't try to move," she said calmly. "You've been in an accident, but you're going to be okay."

An accident?

"She's awake?" Dad barged through the door holding two cups of coffee.

"Yes," Mom said to him. She returned her attention to me. "Do you remember what happened?"

"An accident…?" My voice was scratchy. I hated riding the Rebel in the rain. I usually avoided it at all costs. But last night… I vaguely recalled headlights…and then darkness.

"A car crossed the center line on Bendham Street. You swerved to avoid him and lost control. You slid into a ditch."

"Thank God you were in town and not out on the highway going sixty-five." Dad's tone was tense.

"You were in no condition to be riding last night," Mom added. "We never should've let you walk out the door."

"I see our patient is awake." A pretty woman with flawless cocoa skin and dark hair tugged into a tight bun scooted up to my bedside. "Meg, my name is Aubrey. You were given a mild sedative. You probably feel a bit groggy."

"It was to help with the pain," Mom chimed in. "How are you feeling?"

"Awful."

Aubrey busied herself taking my vitals and jotting notations onto her clipboard. "You could be feeling much worse," my nurse chided. "You got pretty banged up, but you're fortunate it's nothing life-threatening. You have bruised ribs and a fractured wrist. I imagine you've got a pretty bad headache. You have a concussion, and you're awfully lucky you didn't end up with a skull fracture. Often in motorcycle accidents we see serious abrasions but again, you were fortunate."

"Thank God you were wearing riding gear," Dad said.

I had been wearing my leather pants, leather coat, and thick riding boots along with my helmet. No doubt they had saved me from being grated like a chunk of cheese as I slid across the asphalt.

Fuzzy images flashed through my mind. Lights burning overhead as I was wheeled down a hallway… Flashes of people clad in blue scrubs… A white coat… Garbled voices… Between the sedation and the concussion, my thoughts were still fuzzy.

Aubrey spoke with my parents, who cast me worried

glances despite her reassuring smile. I couldn't hear her
murmurings over the pounding in my head. I briefly wondered
if she'd consider slipping me another sedative but then more
memories from the night before began to trickle through my
mind.

Mom had been abusing sleeping pills.

Dad had found out.

Our family was on the verge of shattering, possibly
irrevocably.

Apprehension quickly overshadowed my pain. It was
soothed slightly when I realized Dad's hand rested on the
small of Mom's back. She was leaning in, listening intently to
the nurse.

The moment Aubrey disappeared, Mom came to my side.
She picked up my left hand in hers. It wasn't until then that I
realized my right arm was in a cast. It should've been obvious,
given that the nurse mentioned I had a fractured wrist, but
until that moment I'd been too loopy to notice.

"A doctor will be in to see you soon. Aubrey thinks you'll
be discharged by the end of the day," Dad said.

"If you feel up to going home," Mom added.

"I do."

"I want you to know things will be different," Mom began.
"After you left last night your father and I sat down and had a
talk. A real talk. What you said about Sydney, it hurt. But you
were right. She would hate the way things are. I want to honor
her memory, not destroy our family. I told your father I was
willing to go to counseling."

"Really?" My voice sounded small and hopeful.

"Really," Dad said. "I suggested we also seek marriage
counseling. Your mother agreed."

I looked at my mom. Really looked at her. She looked
exhausted, sure. But she also seemed more lucid than I
remembered her being in a long while.

"Your father was right. I can't go on living the way I've been. It's an insult to Sydney's memory. It's an insult to our family. I got so wrapped up in trying to numb myself, in trying to forget the pain, that I forgot what's really important."

Dad gave me a weak smile. I got the impression that he wanted to believe Mom, but she was going to have to prove herself with more than words.

"Did you talk to Miss Perez?" I asked.

"No, sweetie, not yet," Mom said. "But I will call her soon. After we get you out of here."

"Your mom and I were beginning to work out the details when the policeman showed up at the door."

"Oh, Meg," Mom sighed. "When I saw him standing there, I was so scared. Nothing good ever comes from having a policeman show up on your front steps. I was so afraid we'd lost you. I was so afraid that when I finally realized I needed to be a better mom to you," her voice cracked, "that it was too late."

"The Rebel is totaled," Dad said.

I winced. "I'm sorry."

He waved my apology away. "I don't give a damn about the bike. I never should've let you ride it in the first place. I only wanted you to know you won't be riding it anymore."

"When the insurance check comes in, we'd like you to use it for a down payment on a car," Mom said. "I can't bear the thought of you on a motorcycle ever again."

She gave me a stern look, as if she thought I would argue. She had nothing to worry about.

"We were lucky Luke was there to get you help as quickly as he did," Dad said.

"Luke?" I must've heard wrong. "He wasn't there."

Mom and Dad shared relieved glances.

"He was there," Mom assured me. "He said the two of you had an argument. You left before he could stop you. He followed you, saw the entire thing. He called 911 and stayed with you until the paramedics arrived."

Luke had been there?

"That poor boy," Mom sympathized. "You were unconscious when he got to you. He thought the worst when you were unresponsive. By the time the ambulance arrived he'd found a pulse."

"He rode in the ambulance with you," Dad continued. "He was here until a few hours ago."

"He was muddy and drenched from the storm. I convinced him to go home to clean up," Mom told me. "He didn't want to go. We said we'd call him when you woke up."

"Oh, right," Dad said. "I suppose I ought to do that."

"No," I winced in pain as I shook my head. "I don't want you to call him."

"Meg," Dad said gently, "the boy wants to know that you're okay."

"I think he deserves to know that," Mom agreed. "He was a wreck last night. He really cares about you."

"No, he doesn't."

"I understand you had an argument. But I'm sure you can work through it." Mom gave me a supportive smile. "I know he'll want to get over here as soon as he hears you're awake."

I wanted to scream. How was it that after all this time she chose *now* to go all motherly on me?

"Fine. Tell him I'm okay," I relented. I supposed if he had helped me he deserved that much. "But I do not want to see him."

A sharp knock on the doorframe halted Mom from giving more bewildering advice. We all angled our heads to get a better look at the graying man dressed in a white coat.

"Good morning, I'm Dr. Hammond," he said as he strode into the room. "What do you think about getting out of here today?"

"I think I like that idea a lot," I admitted.

My parents both stepped to the side to let Dr. Hammond's examination begin.

• • •

I saw the flowers, what looked like an enormous floating bouquet, come through the door before I saw the guy behind them. Luke lowered the vase full of colorful tulips. I realized he also carried a plain pink gift bag. He set both on my desk.

"I brought you every classic movie I could find. I thought you'd like something to do while you recover." He gave me a forced smile.

"What are you doing here?" My throat constricted and tears instantly threatened. My body buzzed with conflicting emotions. I missed him but I didn't want him here. My anger had faded to an aching sadness I couldn't shake. "I told Dad to let you know I'm okay. I didn't want you stopping by."

His smile faded.

I shifted against my stack of pillows. My head felt better but the aching in my ribs had yet to cease. I was grateful to Dr. Hammond for the prescription of painkillers he'd sent home with me.

"I know. I won't stay long. I just needed to see you. Had to see for myself that you're okay." He dropped onto the chair. He leaned forward, elbows resting on knees. "How are you doing?"

He looked put together in his dark jeans and long-sleeve white thermal. But the dark crescents under his eyes, the droop of his shoulders, told another story. He was exhausted. As was I.

"I'm doing okay," I admitted. "Kylie and Francesca just left."

"You scared the hell out of me, Meg." His voice trembled

as his eyes cut into me. My stomach twisted, noting the pain in his gaze. "When I saw you slide off the road, it felt like my heart exploded in my chest. I pulled over, and it felt like it took forever to get to you. When I reached you, you were so still. I thought I'd lost you. I never should've let you leave after our fight. I wish I could go back and change that entire conversation."

He leaned forward, reaching for my hand. I tugged it away. His expression rippled with emotions. He had no right to tear at my heart the way he did.

"I'd rather hear the truth than a lie. Using me to make Jaclyn back off, that's one thing. At least you were upfront about that. Using me because you knew your parents would find me *unacceptable*? *Unfit* to be your girlfriend. That's just wrong." I tried to mask how much that *hurt*. "But it worked for you so. Yeah. You got what you want. You get to go to your camp."

"Forget about the camp."

"Why?"

"I'm not going. What happened between you and me, it stopped being about the camp a long time ago."

His dejected look made me want to throw the vase of flowers at him. "You put me through all of that, and you're not even going to go? What was the point of it all then? You're not even making sense." A sob tore at me, and I gasped, trying to calm the raging pain in my ribs. I knew I was being irrational, but he destroyed what we'd been building…for what? Or maybe I'd been wrong and we had nothing to start with.

"Nutmeg—" He moved toward me again.

"Don't." My voice quaked. I desperately did not want to cry anymore. My battered ribs couldn't take the abuse. "Don't call me that."

"The fight we had, it never should've happened." He spoke haltingly, his voice cracking. "I wish I could say more than that. I wish I could explain what really happened."

"What really happened?" I shook my head. "I was there. I recall what happened."

"That's not what I mean."

"Then what do you mean?"

He raked a hand through his hair, leaving it as chaotic as the expression he wore. "I can't get into it. Not yet."

"More secrets? Or just an excuse?"

I wanted to scrub that dejected look off his face. What right did he have to look so miserable? He was the one who had schemed, had lied, had used me.

"Luke," I angrily scrubbed a few tears away, "I'm grateful that you were there for me the other night. I'm grateful that you called for help. Other than that, I really have nothing else to say to you. I think you should leave."

He ground out a sigh. "I made a mistake. I never meant to hurt you. I didn't think the blackmail through. I didn't know you. You didn't know me. The idea came to me and I ran with it without considering the consequences."

"Actions always have consequences."

He nodded as he got to his feet. My heart twisted into a tangled knot when I saw the shimmer in his eyes. "I guess we've both learned that the hard way," he said, his voice raspy. "Just remember I'm not the only one who pulled off a reckless stunt without thinking it through."

He slipped out the door, not waiting for a response.

Chapter Twenty-Five

LUKE

Gabe's laugh wasn't at all amused. "Damn, kid. When you said you got yourself into a mess, you weren't kidding around."

"Yeah." Wasn't a whole lot more I could say. I slouched down on the bench, scanning the parking lot for Adam. I needed to be done with this phone call before he showed up. He asked if I'd meet him at the field for some practice time. I was sure it was just an excuse to get my mind off Meg. I appreciated it but really didn't feel like throwing around a ball right now.

The last few days I'd been wallowing.

Today? I was trying to pick myself up and brush myself off. I was off to a rocky start. I woke up determined to make things right with Meg. But as the day wore on, I realized the odds were against me.

I wasn't going to give up. But I definitely needed help.

"I feel like this is somewhat my fault." Gabe sighed. "When I told you to get out from under Dad, I had no idea you'd go to such extreme measures. I thought the training camp was a great idea. But bringing Meg into it…"

"Was one of the stupidest things I've ever done," I finished for him. "I know. I'd give anything to take it back."

"You can't." Gabe said bluntly. "You need to figure out where to go from here."

"I was hoping you could help with that."

"I figured."

"I did what Jaclyn wanted so she wouldn't turn Meg in. Meg's barely out of the hospital. She hates me and will probably never speak to me again." With good reason. "She has no idea that Jaclyn knows *everything*. I couldn't tell her. That's the last thing I want to throw at her right now."

Stressing about the possibility of jail time hardly made for a peaceful recovery.

Going to her house had probably been a mistake. But seeing her fly off the road, seeing her lying there so still? It had been the worst moment of my life. I'd never felt so helpless, so scared.

I wanted to explain what really happened the night of the accident. I wanted her to know that she was worth so much more to me than that damn camp. But I couldn't do that yet. Not when Jaclyn was still a threat.

"Your ex is a ticking time bomb."

"I know."

Everything happened so fast the night of the accident. I'd been desperate to give Jaclyn what she wanted to keep Meg safe. I reacted on impulse, not thinking it through. I broke Meg's heart. Caused her accident.

The worst part of it all?

I did it with no guarantee that Jaclyn wouldn't turn around and use the information she had anyway. Sure, she *said* we had a deal.

But I trusted her about as much as I trusted any other

venomous snake.

"We need to come up with a way to neutralize her."

"I know." I got up and started to pace. "I can't let Jaclyn take Meg down because of me. This is my fault. If I'd just left her alone that night at the school… If I hadn't blackmailed her… Jaclyn went after her because she knows how much Meg means to me. It's my fault she started digging around."

"You do realize," Gabe said, "that Meg isn't entirely guiltless. She did paint the school."

"And I was at the water tower. As far as I'm concerned, that makes me guilty, too."

"It's not like we can pay her off," Gabe muttered. "Jaclyn wouldn't care about the money. There's got to be another way."

"I have to do something." My voice shook with frustration. "I have to find a way to make this right."

"I'll do some checking around."

"Checking what?"

"Let me worry about details. You've got enough to deal with right now. Trust me on this."

We disconnected, and I dropped back down on the bench. I didn't see Adam yet. I propped my elbows on my knees and rested my face in my hands. My eyelids grated like sandpaper. I felt like I hadn't slept in a year.

I'd seen Jaclyn in the parking lot at school. She barely glanced my way. If she felt bad about the accident at all, it would probably pass sooner rather than later. I'd been given a reprieve, but I wasn't stupid enough to think it would last indefinitely.

"Hey, dude. Naptime is over."

I lifted my head and struggled for my game face.

Adam eyed me up. "You don't look so good." He dropped down next to me. "What happened the other night? Julia stopped by to see Meg. She said the two of you were over."

"Did she say why?"

He slid me a cautious look. "Uh, I guess she told Julia you two just weren't good together. Could've fooled me though. You guys seemed fine the last time I saw you. What happened?"

"It's a long story. Too long to get into."

"I've got time," he offered.

"I did something stupid."

"Yeah?" Like a good friend, he sounded skeptical. "What did you do?"

"Something so stupid I can't even talk about it."

He slapped my shoulder. "If you change your mind, you know where to find me. Get your ass up. Our star pitcher does not belong on the bench."

I realized Adam had scrounged up a few of our teammates. They were jogging across the field. Leo was there, Colton, Dillon. Not enough guys for a game, but enough to get a pretty intense practice in.

When we wrapped up a few hours later I was grateful to the guys for helping me kill some time. I couldn't help but think that Meg's house was within walking distance from the park. I could be there in five minutes.

Not a good idea.

We piled into the dugout to load up our bat bags.

Out of habit I checked my phone, hoping for a text from Meg. Of course she hadn't tried to get a hold of me.

But Gabe had. And that was almost as good.

Gabe: *I've got what you need. Call me.*

Adam nudged me. "Did you hear that? We're going out for pizza. Want to ride with me?"

Heart hammering, I slipped my phone into my pocket.

"Can't make it but thanks."

I took off at a jog toward my truck. I heard someone,

probably Leo, call after me. I didn't have time to see what he wanted.

Once I was in my driver's seat and had some privacy, I gave Gabe a call.

"What've you got?" I asked.

"You're going to want to see this for yourself. What's that little diner you like?"

"Maebelle's?"

"Can you be there in half an hour?"

Hell, I could be there in ten minutes.

"Yes," I said. "See you then."

• • •

I ordered a root beer as I waited for my brother to arrive. I contemplated onion rings, but it just wasn't the same if I couldn't share them with Meg.

I jabbed at the ice with my straw. I hoped whatever he had was as good as he thought it was.

I'd dropped in at Meg's normal lunch table today. I was hoping her friends would give me an update. Francesca told me Meg was no longer my concern and asked me to leave.

I was surprised when Kylie rushed up to my locker after school. She told me Meg was doing okay, but she'd be out of school for at least a week. She also shared that Rick and Marion had some kind of breakthrough. Kylie said Meg was optimistic that her parents were going to stay together. But they still had a rocky road ahead.

I didn't want to add any more obstacles. If Meg was arrested, I didn't know how her family would handle that.

I had to make sure that didn't happen.

I shouldn't have antagonized Jaclyn the last time I saw her. That was like poking a viper.

"Sorry I'm late." Gabe slid into the booth. "Traffic." He

set his briefcase on the table. "I'd give you a lecture on all the reasons it was wrong to blackmail Meg, but I think you're being hard enough on yourself already."

I nodded. "What did you find?"

"Good idea. Let's get down to business. I poked around a bit at the office. George Winters isn't exactly popular there. One of the underlings was more than happy to dish some dirt. He's probably doing it to brown nose, thinking it'll earn him points with the family. Or a promotion. But it got the job done."

I waited impatiently as he popped his briefcase open. "Do you remember a teacher by the name of Mr. Taylor?"

"Yeah." I scoffed. "He was young, a first-year teacher. The girls wouldn't shut up about him. I was kind of dating Meredith at the time. She was always blabbing about how hot he was. What does this have to do with Jaclyn?"

I took in Gabe's smug smile.

"No." My heart slammed around as I leaned forward and lowered my voice. "She had an affair with a teacher?" Would it really be that big of a surprise? Nope. I wouldn't put anything past her.

"She didn't have an affair. But not for her lack of trying." He pulled out a manila envelope and shook the contents free. "Check this out."

"Order for Protection?" I clenched my jaw. "Did he hurt her?" The girl was proving to be a crazy pants bitch but there were some things guys just didn't do.

"Read the details carefully."

I did and felt my eyes bulge.

"The order is *against* her."

"That it is. Little brother, your ex is a certifiable stalker." He shifted, looking pleased with himself. "It gets better."

"How could it possibly get better? This is *golden*!"

"Eileen has no idea. George took care of everything,"

Gabe explained.

"Eileen would come undone if she knew her teen daughter was stalking a teacher."

"As far as I can tell, it's all in the past. But that could be in part because George paid this guy a substantial amount of money to leave town."

"I assume Eileen doesn't know that, either?"

Gabe's smug smile was my answer. "Take this to Jaclyn. She's not going to want her mom to find out any of this."

"Or her friends," I muttered. Jaclyn had too much pride to let anyone know she'd thrown herself at someone. Thrown herself so repeatedly that the OFP was needed "How did you get this?"

"I told you, I'm not proud of it, but I've learned a lot from Dad."

I needed no further explanation.

"The way I see it, your problem is twofold," Gabe said. "This will neutralize Jaclyn, just like we wanted. The cops are another matter entirely. The rewards aren't just going to go away. Have you given any thought to how you want to handle that?"

"Yeah." I jabbed at the ice cubes again. "I'm glad you asked."

Chapter Twenty-Six

MEG

I paused in front of Miss Perez's door. It was closed. She was probably with someone. I should come back.

I twisted around and nearly collided with her.

"Good morning. How are you?" Her eyes scanned over me. "You look good. All things considered."

"Yeah." I held my injured hand up. "I'm doing okay."

"I just got out of a staff meeting." She shuffled the files she carried to her other arm and stuffed her hand in her pocket, producing a key. "I assume you're here to talk. I have some time. I could write a pass for you if you end up late for first hour."

She opened her door but before stepping inside she ripped the reward poster off the wall. "These can all come down. Finally."

"What? Why?" I glanced down the long hallway where they were dotted about.

"Whoever did it turned themselves in."

My blood turned to ice. Had someone turned *me* in? Is that what she meant? I pressed a hand against the wall to keep myself upright. My head still echoed with an ache from the accident. My wrist throbbed. My Rebel was totaled. The old adage "When it rains it pours" spilled into my head. On top of everything else—the accident, losing Luke—was I going to finally have to pay for this, too?

While I knew it would only be fair, I didn't think I could face it. My parents were finally willing to seek help. Our family was on the verge of a new normal. This could ruin everything.

And it would be *all* my fault.

"Meg?" She looped her arm through mine. "Let's get you inside so you can sit down. You don't look too good. Maybe you came back to school too early."

She led me to my usual chair. I slumped into it.

"Who did it? The vandalism?" My voice quaked. I waited for her to give me a look of sheer disappointment, telling me I knew the answer to that.

"All I know is that it was a student. He or she is a minor, they had a lawyer. Everything is very hush-hush."

A lawyer?

I pressed my hands against my burning cheeks. My fingers were ice-cold. I happened to know someone who had a lawyer for a father. But he wouldn't.

Would he?

"What will happen to this person?"

Miss Perez winced. "Mr. Prichard has been furious about this incident. In past meetings he was adamant that if he found out it was a student, they would be expelled."

Expelled?

"So," she cocked her head to the side, "what would you like to talk about?"

It took me a moment to round up my scattered thoughts.

"I just stopped by to thank you. I know you've spoken

with Mom a few times. She said you suggested a therapist for her and my dad. They already made an appointment. They're going to go together."

"I was more than happy to do it. I know it's been a long, painful journey for your family. I think a therapist will lead them down the road to closure."

I nodded. "I hope so."

"And you?" she pressed. "Your mom mentioned you were having a bit of boy trouble. Care to talk about it?"

Trouble? I felt like I was in the midst of a catastrophe.

"There's really nothing to say. He lied to me." I pinched the bridge of my nose. "That's not exactly true. He kept something from me. Something big."

"Is it possible he had a good reason?"

"*He* thought so."

"You clearly disagree," she said gently. "I don't suppose you want to elaborate?"

I shook my head.

She leaned back. "Without knowing the situation, there's not a lot I can say. I do suggest you try to keep in mind that sometimes things spin out of control. Sometimes something that seems harmless blows up in our faces."

I could completely relate to that.

A water tower at the edge of town could *attest* to that.

How was Luke any more at fault than I was?

Maybe this could be one of those rare times when two wrongs could make a right.

I glanced at the clock ticking over her head. I didn't have a lot of time before class and there was something I needed to do.

I slid out of my chair. "I really shouldn't miss first hour my first day back. Thanks for meeting with me on such short notice."

"It's my pleasure. Check in with me soon, okay?"

I agreed and then I was rushing down the hall.

I went to the front doors and moved onto the steps that led out of the building. I studied the parking lot across the street. Mom had dropped me off this morning, and I'd gone straight to Miss Perez. Now, as I looked for Luke's Navigator, it was conspicuously absent.

Julia's locker was near Luke's. I swerved my way through the crowd, grateful to find her still there.

"Julia?"

"Meg." Her eyes widened and she pulled me into a gentle hug. "I'm so glad you're back."

"Thanks. Um, have you seen Luke?"

"Not yet. Maybe he's sick?" She shrugged. "Adam hasn't said anything. I don't know if he's checked in with him or not."

I wasn't sure what to make of the news. Surely, if Luke had been expelled, people would know by now, wouldn't they?

My first few hours dragged by. By the time I stuffed my books in my locker, ready for lunch, I was frazzled.

"Meg."

I turned around and Francesca grabbed me by the shoulders.

"I'm so glad to see you," she said dramatically. She glanced around before leaning in to whisper, "There's a rumor going around that the vandal was caught. I knew you were supposed to be coming to school today, but you weren't at your locker this morning. I've been *freaking* out." Her hands slid away and she gave me some space.

"I was in Miss Perez's office. *Someone* turned themselves in."

"Who...?" Her eyes grew wide. "Did...?"

I shrugged. "I don't know. But who else possibly would have? He's not here today."

"Meg," her tone turned serious, "if he took the fall for you, this is huge. This means no more posters around the school. No more front page stories. No more wondering if some witness is going to materialize out of thin air."

"I know."

"You need to find out what's going on." She grabbed my uninjured wrist and gave me a tug. "Come on."

"Where are we going?"

"Who needs lunch? You need to clear things up with Luke."

• • •

Francesca parked on the street. If Luke's mom was home, I didn't want to have a run-in with her. I hurried up the driveway and looped around to the backside of the house. Maybe he wasn't even here.

He could've taken a skip day. He might be at the coast. Or maybe his family decided on a last minute vacation.

For all I knew, the boy could be in Rome.

There was only one way to find out. I hit send and waited for the phone to ring.

"Meg?" he sounded wary.

"Hey."

"Hi. I'm a little surprised to hear from you."

"I think we need to talk."

"Okay…?"

"In person."

He hesitated. "Yeah. Where do you want to meet?"

"In the gazebo? I would've thrown a rock at your window, but you know, that's kind of a cliché."

His face appeared in his window. "I'll be right down."

I met him on the backside of the house. "Is there something you want to tell me?" I asked.

"There's a lot I want to tell you."

We wandered toward the gazebo and took a seat.

"Did you take the fall for me?"

"Yeah."

"Why would you do that?" I collapsed against the gazebo's railing, the weight of his admission hitting me hard. I had suspected—I mean, who else could it have been—but hearing him say it still stunned me.

"The night of the accident, things got complicated. That night, what I wanted to tell you was that I've completely fallen for you. Instead, everything imploded."

He explained to me what went down between him and Jaclyn.

"I was trying to protect you that night. I swear. Mom knew you and I were going to talk. Dad offered me the camp. I had no intention of taking it. I'd given up on the idea a while ago. But then Jaclyn showed up...and everything spiraled. When she wanted me to end things with you, it was the first thing that came to mind."

I was still reeling from the news that Jaclyn found out.

"Are you expelled?"

Luke scoffed. "I feel like a hypocrite. I always grumble about Dad getting people out of trouble when they don't deserve it. But Gabe worked some magic. I got off pretty light. I'm suspended through the week, had to pay a hefty fine, which Gabe covered because he felt like he was partly to blame. I'm a minor so my name won't be in the paper. Mr. Prichard and the superintendent know it was me, but they aren't allowed to share the info with anyone without violating confidentiality." He shrugged. "I have to fulfill ten hours of community service. It could've been a lot worse."

What he meant was that if I'd gone down for this, the punishment *would've* been a lot worse. Money and prestige talk.

"Thank you. I can't believe you did this for me." I grimaced. "Even though you confessed, Jaclyn could still take everything to the cops." What if Luke had gone through all of this for nothing?

"Already got it covered. I don't want you to worry about a thing." I gave him a questioning look. "Let's just say when Gabe works his magic, he really works it."

"Your parents?"

He winced. "Not happy. Gabe spun some excuse about my behavior being an act of rebellion. He suggested they stop trying to micromanage my future. I don't know if they'll back off, but I think they bought it."

It took my brain several minutes to absorb everything. I was grateful Luke had Gabe. Dragging his dad into this would've indebted Luke to him in ways I didn't even want to think about.

"Would you have told me? About your original plan if she hadn't cornered you into it?"

Conflicting emotions flashed across his face. "Honestly? No. I didn't see the point. I realized how stupid it was. I didn't want you to find out. The fact that you're different is what I love most about you. You're not one of those cookie cutter girls, trying to be the same as everyone else."

I fidgeted with the hem of my sweater.

"Is there any chance we can move past this?" he asked. "I want to make things right between us. I made a mistake. You can relate to that, can't you?"

"Yeah," I admitted, "I know a little bit about things spiraling out of control."

"Then please tell me you understand that I didn't mean to hurt you."

"I get it," I said. "I don't like it but I do understand."

What he had done had hurt. But I did believe him when he said that was never his intention. I knew what it was like to regret something. I also knew life was too short to hold on to a grudge.

"I think I've made my feelings for you pretty clear," Luke said. "But I have no idea how you feel after everything that's happened."

He'd been so open with me I decided it was only fair to reciprocate.

"I don't know when it happened," I began, "but somewhere along the way, I realized it's pretty hard not to love you."

His adorable dimples greeted me. "Yeah?"

"Yeah."

I leaned in, slid my hand around the back of his neck, and pressed my lips against his. It was a soft kiss, sweet, and full of promises for more.

Epilogue

MEG

Over the next month Mom was true to her word. She met with the therapist Miss Perez recommended. She still had bad days. Lots of them. But as the weeks went by, as she learned to cope on her own, the bad days seemed to happen less and less.

Dad had been serious about seeing a marriage counselor. They had a standing date every Tuesday afternoon with the same therapist that Mom saw individually.

Mom had made a point of spending time with me every day. Whether it be breakfast, a few minutes after school to hear about my day, or a prolonged conversation at dinnertime. Dad noticed, and he definitely approved.

We had a long way to go before we felt like a "normal" family again. Maybe, without Sydney, we never would. We had a long road to recovery ahead of us, but we were all walking it together.

Mom and Dad adored Luke. Who could blame them?

"Have fun tonight," Mom said.

Dad grinned and added the obligatory, "But not too much fun."

I rolled my eyes, enjoying the cheesy banter I hadn't even realized I'd been missing out on. "Thanks. You two have a nice evening."

I grabbed my purse and darted onto the porch. I was anxious to see my boyfriend. I didn't want to waste a minute of this evening. I knew if he came through the front door my parents would tangle him up in a conversation that would feel like it would never end.

He was halfway up the sidewalk when I emerged. The heels of my black buckled boots clicked against the pavement as I hopped off the bottom step.

He froze in place when he saw me. For a moment I felt self-conscious. Then his familiar dimpled grin edged onto his face as he took in my appearance from head to toe. He didn't bother to hide that he liked what he saw.

I glanced down at myself, taking in the turquoise sweater that Mom said set off my hair. It hung slightly off the shoulders, giving me the edginess I still desired. My white skinny jeans fit like they'd been made for me. My boots felt comfortable and familiar.

"Mom and I went shopping."

"I see that. I like this new look. What's the occasion?" he teased.

"Oh, you know, nothing special," I teased back. "Just a one-month anniversary dinner."

"Well, I like it." He pressed a kiss to my cheek, and I sighed happily.

He escorted me to his SUV and helped me into the seat. Since the accident he'd become my self-appointed chauffer.

"We have reservations at Natalia's at seven," he told me. "You can order the lobster ravioli and enjoy every bite of it. I was thinking for dessert, the tiramisu?"

"Sounds perfect," I said. "Although I'd be just as happy going out for a burger."

"I know," he agreed. "That's why I want to take you somewhere nice."

I assumed he was driving aimlessly, chewing up time before our reservation. I spotted the water tower looming in the distance. The sun was setting behind it. The sky was streaked with molten gold. I thought it looked like a glimpse into Heaven.

I was lost in my thoughts, comforting thoughts of Sydney, knowing she was healthy and happy, in a better place.

He pulled over to the side of the road.

My mural stood watch over the town. The city hadn't decided what to do with it yet. A surprising number of residents had spoken up. They appreciated the way it spruced up the crummy old tower.

As happy as that made me, I wasn't about to return to my old habit.

"What are we doing here?"

"I wanted to talk, but not in the restaurant."

That grabbed my attention. I twisted in my seat to fully face him. "Is something wrong?"

"I talked to my dad today, finally," he said. "I told him law school wasn't for me."

"And…?"

"He laughed at me. Then he yelled. Then he threatened." He shook his head. "It went pretty much the way I expected it to go."

"I'm sorry."

"Don't be. I'm not. I've been thinking it's for the best. I talked to Miss Perez last week. You were right about her." He smiled. "She helped me look at my options. And there's always the chance that Coach will be able to line up some scouts since I'm not going to Colorado. But if that doesn't work out for me,

I'll figure something else out. She's pretty sure my grades will help me qualify for an academic scholarship. Dad was always so hard on me about my grades. I guess it's paid off."

"That's good, right?"

"It is good. Knowing I'll be able to get out from under my parents, it's freeing." He swung his attention back to me and gave me a teasing grin. "Miss Perez said it will also look good on my transcripts to have the Ecology Club listed. It will round things out for when I start applying to colleges."

"You're joining the Ecology Club?"

He grinned. "Why not?"

I smiled but my eyes floated back to the tower.

"Hey, Nutmeg." He twirled a lock of my hair around his finger and I turned to face him. "I know you miss it. But you need to move forward from here. No looking back."

"I know." It was hard, but he was right.

"I have something for you." He pulled a small box out of the armrest. "As you can see, it's not a pony. But it is a bit shiny."

He held out the long, thin, burgundy box to me. His eyes sparkled and those adorable dimples about did me in.

"Open it."

I did as requested and gasped at what I saw.

"Luke." His name came out as a reverent whisper. Never in my life had I received a gift that was so perfect.

The pendant that rested against a bed of black velvet made my heart skip a beat. I lifted a finger, touching the edge. The center of the pendant was a heart, encrusted with rubies. From the heart sprouted two wings. The diamond chips comprising the wings sparkled as he shifted the box in his hands.

"Do you like it?"

"I absolutely love it."

"I know you painted because it made you feel closer to

your sister. Now that you've given it up I wanted you to feel like you were keeping a little piece of Sydney with you, no matter where you go, or what you do."

He pulled the delicate chain from the box. I instinctively leaned forward so he could clasp it around my neck. When it was in place I leaned back again. My fingers brushed against the quarter-sized piece of jewelry. "I don't think I'm ever going to take it off."

My admission made his smile even bigger.

My smile faltered. "I'm sorry. I didn't get you anything."

I wasn't well versed in the rituals of one-month anniversaries.

Fake dating Luke had been nice. Dating him for real was so much better.

"I didn't want you to get me anything," he said. "If it makes you feel better, don't think of it as an anniversary gift. Let's think of it as an apology gift."

"Apology?" I echoed.

"An apology for blackmailing you. I can't stop thinking about how stupid that was. I'm sorry."

"Don't be. I'm not. If you hadn't blackmailed me, I'd never have gotten to know you. And if you hadn't forced me to play by the rules, we wouldn't be sitting here today."

"The rules." Luke smirked and shook his head. "They didn't work out the way I thought they would."

"No?" I twisted around, squeezing myself between the seats. I spotted the green notebook sticking out from under his floor mat. I grabbed it and plopped back onto my seat.

He groaned. "What could you possibly be writing in that thing?"

I tugged out the red pen he'd crammed in the spiral binding. I quickly scrawled a sentence at the bottom of an already filled up page.

Meg and Luke have no more rules.

He flashed a wry smile. "I like some of our rules."

"Me too," I admitted. "But I'd rather do something because it's a choice."

"Good point." He leaned in, his breath whispering across my cheek. "And if I choose to kiss you now?"

Despite all the times Luke had kissed me, he could still make my heart hopscotch in my chest. "I'd say you're making an excellent choice."

He pulled the notebook from my hands, tossed it on the backseat, and showed me just how much he appreciated my answer.

Acknowledgments

There are no words to describe how grateful I am to my sons, Zack and Nick. Writing is such a time-consuming process. You've never complained about how many hours I spend locked away, even when it takes time away from you. I appreciate your support and your excitement over the years as my writing career has progressed. I love you more than you will ever know.

Thank you to my family and friends. You have always been there for me, always supported me. I am so incredibly lucky to have each and every one of you.

To my readers, old and new, thank you for choosing to spend your time with the characters I've created.

Stacy Abrams and Alexa May, I am so grateful that you saw the potential in my manuscript. Your input on this book was invaluable. Thank you for helping me to mold it into the version it is today. I would also like to thank everyone behind the scenes at Entangled Publishing. I feel so fortunate to be working with such a wonderful team.

About the Author

Amity lives in beautiful northern Minnesota with her two sons, two persnickety cats, and the world's sweetest Rottweiler.

She has a degree in elementary education and worked in that field for ten years before deciding to self-publish. It was the best decision she's ever made.

If she's not writing, or spending time with her boys, she's most likely reading.

Visit Amity online at: http://authoramityhope.blogspot.com/

Discover more of Entangled Teen Crush's books...

BREAKAWAY

a *Corrigan Falls Raiders* novel by Cate Cameron

Eighteen-year-old NHL player Logan Balanchuk came to Corrigan Falls to distract himself from his career-ending injury. He doesn't want to even hear the word "hockey," so when he meets Dawn, a beautiful, free-spirited girl who goes skinny-dipping instead of watching the draft, he's intrigued. But she's already done her time as a hockey player's girlfriend—now she wants to live her own life and have her own adventures...

TAMING THE REBEL

an *Endless Summer* novel by Dawn Klehr

Rebel Hart should be at home taking care of her father after his breakup with his boyfriend, not tromping through the woods at summer camp. He's had his heart broken beyond repair, and the way she sees it, there's only one person to blame—the boyfriend's son. So when that infuriatingly gorgeous quarterback turns up at the same camp, she plans to make him pay.

ARTIFICIAL SWEETHEARTS
a *North Pole, Minnesota* novel by Julie Hammerle

It's not chemistry between Tinka Foster and Sam Anderson that made them agree to fake date. With her parents trying to set her up with an annoying pro-track golf student, and intentionally single Sam's family pressuring him to find a girlfriend, they could both use a drama-free summer. So it's not his muscular arms and quick wit that makes Tinka suggest they tell everyone they're both taken. Definitely not. And it's not butterflies that makes a kiss for appearances go on way too long. So there's no way fake couldn't be perfect.

BLACKMAIL BOYFRIEND
a *Boyfriend Chronicles* novel by Chris Cannon

Haley Patterson, honor student, has had a crush on popular, golden boy Bryce Colton for ages. But then she hears a rumor— Bryce is telling everyone that he hooked up with *her*. With Haley's reputation taking a serious nose-dive, she gives Bryce a choice: be her boyfriend for a month, or face the angry, cage-fighting boyfriend of the girl he actually *did* hook up with. Now Bryce is being blackmailed by a girl who has two three-legged dogs and lives on the other side of town. Can something so fake turn into something real?

CPSIA information can be obtained
at www.ICGtesting.com
Printed in the USA
BVOW06s2155150118
505351BV00001B/5/P